Why Did You Die IN THE PARK?

Sharon 1/11

A Marge Christensen Mystery

Why Did You Die
IN THE PARK?

To Mystery Readers Everywhere!
Patricia K. Batta

PATRICIA K. BATTA

LILLIMAR PUBLISHING
Traverse City, Michigan

Lillimar Publishing
Traverse City, Mich.

Batta, Patricia K.

Why did you die in the park? : a Marge Christensen mystery / Patricia K. Batta — Traverse City, Mich. : Lillimar Publishing, c2009.

p. ; cm.

ISBN: 978-0-9797883-1-4

1. Christensen, Marge (Fictitious character)—Fiction. 2. Widows—Fiction. 3. Friendship—Fiction. 4. Bellevue (Wash.)—Fiction. 5. Mystery fiction. I. Title.

PS3602.A898 W49 2009 2009922722
813/.6—dc22 0905

Printed in the United States of America
10 9 8 7 6 5 4 3 2 1

BOOK DESIGN BY TO THE POINT SOLUTIONS
www.tothepointsolutions.com

In honor of my mother, May E. McAllister,
who, in addition to many other things,
taught me the meaning of perseverance.

ACKNOWLEDGMENTS

THANK YOU TO MY fourth-grade teacher, who ignited in me a love of writing that would not be extinguished, and to my English professor at Northwestern Michigan College, Al Shumsky, for giving me the courage to persevere.

Still, it was many years later, in a Seattle writer's group facilitated by Roberta Jean Bryant, that I began to truly believe I could do it. Thank you to Jean for her inspired leadership, and recently for her honest and forthright criticism without which the series never would have been marketable.

Thanks also are due to Nancy Bordine, Barb Smith, Roger Rowen, Barb Wallace, and Jody Clark, my current writer's group at the Traverse City, Michigan, library. Their encouragement, comments, and suggestions helped me complete the books I had been laboring over for so long.

And finally, many thanks to Mary Jo Zazueta of To The Point Solutions, who helped put the final touches on *What Did You Do Before Dying?* and *Why Did You Die In the Park?* She took the pain out of publishing.

Also, thank you to Denise Glesser of Progressive Book Marketing for her enthusiasm in promoting the books.

Why Did You Die IN THE PARK?

CHAPTER 1

"DON'T BE SILLY," Marge told herself, scoffing at the sudden urge to grab her backpack and flee to the safety of her apartment. Forcing herself to remain calm, she took a deep breath, placed her sketchpad on the log, stood up, and started down the incline, carefully planting her feet with each step so she wouldn't slip on the soggy leaves that blanketed the ground. She crouched down and slowly moved aside some low branches to get a better look at the mound of damp brown earth, freshly exposed roots, and broken twigs that were only a few feet from the well-worn path. "Odd," she muttered, frowning. "What could have caused this?"

Shrugging, she turned back toward the log to resume her drawing. As she did, a patch of blue caught her eye. Denim? It looked fresh and clean—not like something that had moldered with the leaves over the winter. A flash-back from a little over a year ago, when she had opened the garage door to see the horror of her husband's lifeless body slumped in the front seat of his BMW, jumped into her mind. Something that didn't belong. Something that didn't make sense. Like now. The urge to flee returned.

"No, not like now," Marge said aloud, shaking her head to emphasize the difference and to erase the memory. "That isn't a body. It's just a piece of clothing." The refusal of her feet to move was all that kept her standing there. She took a deep breath and let the musty, sweet smell of last year's decaying leaves calm her. As she exhaled, a slight rustle to her left caught her attention. She peered through the overgrowth and nearly laughed when the image of a big brown bear sprang into her vivid imagination. It must be the wind in the trees, since no wild creatures were likely to lurk in Bellevue, Washington's Kelsey Creek Park. And, if one of the tame animals had escaped from the adjacent farm it was more apt to need help than to be feared.

Marge leaned toward the blue cloth to get a closer look. After all, a scrap of material was no more threatening than a noise in the woods. "So, don't be silly," she repeated. The squeak in her voice would have been funny if her heart hadn't been thudding so hard.

Reaching over with the pencil she still clutched in her hand, she lifted the branches in front of the denim. Her head swam. She took an involuntary step back and managed to turn and take a few steps before her stomach revolted.

The renewed rustling of the wind drifted off into a soft giggle that barely penetrated her consciousness. When her stomach stopped heaving, Marge got up and looked toward the sky. "Why me, God?" she cried. "Isn't once enough?" She had to close her eyes and take several deep cleansing breaths before she could make her rubbery legs retrace her footprints back to her backpack. With trembling hands she pulled out the cell phone and, without even thinking, dialed the number she had called so many times a year ago.

"Detective Peterson, please," she croaked.

"I'm sorry, he's unavailable at the moment. May I take a message or give you his voice mail?"

Annoyance surprised her. She pushed it aside. She should have learned Detective Peterson wouldn't be available whenever she called. "No . . . yes . . . I just found . . . a body," she managed to get out. A clear picture of what she had actually seen flashed through her mind, making her stomach turn over again. "Well . . . actually . . . I found a hand." The line was silent. "Hello . . . hello?" Marge cried.

"What is your name, please?" The voice was hard.

"Marge Christensen," she said.

"Where are you?"

"I'm in Kelsey Creek Park."

"Which part of the park?"

"I'm a little ways off a nature trail, about half a mile east of the parking lot and not far from some wooden steps in the trail." Marge looked around desperately for more landmarks; but without success.

"What makes you think you saw a hand?"

Marge gritted her teeth. "I don't *think* I saw a hand. I *saw* a hand sticking out of the ground." She could hear a disbelieving "Oh, really!" in the sigh that came over the line.

"All right, calm down. Help is on the way." The voice was stern when it added, "Stay right where you are until it gets there."

"I'm not going anywhere," Marge said. The prospect of being alone with the hand brought back the shakes. She grabbed the phone with both hands. "Don't leave me here," she pleaded.

"Don't worry. I'll remain on the line until the police arrive. Tell me, why didn't you call 911?"

The unexpected question quelled the panic more quickly than any soothing words could have. Marge eased her grip on the small phone and frowned. Why *had* she turned to Detective Peterson instead of the more obvious emergency number? "I have no idea," she said. "I guess because I know Detective Peterson my first thought was to call him."

"How do you know Detective Peterson?"

By now Marge had recovered her wits enough to realize the woman on the other end of the line might be making conversation to take her mind off her gruesome discovery. Either that or she didn't believe Marge for a minute and wanted to keep her in place until the police arrived.

The words came hard, but Marge managed to answer. "He investigated my husband's death last year."

"Really?" The calm assurance gave way to surprise. After a moment of silence the woman continued, "Mrs. Christensen, could you give me your address and phone number, please? And tell me, what brought you to Kelsey Creek Park from Newport Hills?"

Marge paused, confused. Newport Hills? Then she realized the entire police department knew the details of Gene's death, since it was the only murder in the Bellevue area in 1997. She had made quite a name for herself when she refused to accept the verdict of suicide and had pestered Detective Peterson until he reopened the investigation. But the police would not know she had sold the house and had since moved to Kelsey Creek Apartments. Marge corrected the information about where she lived.

As Marge explained why she was in the park and what she saw when she lifted the bush, the scream of sirens penetrated the quiet of the woods. The sirens grew louder and louder until they stopped in mid-screech, filling the air with silence. "I think the police have arrived," Marge said. "It sounds like they are in the parking lot."

"They'll be with you soon. Do you have anything to draw their attention?"

Marge looked around. She picked up her backpack but dropped it when she couldn't think of anything in it that would help. Voices called from two directions, followed by the trampling and shuffling of feet on the trail.

"I'm here!" she tried to shout. Her voice felt barely louder than the wind. She'd have to do better than that.

"Should I stay on the line or are you okay?"

"Thank you, I think I'll be okay," Marge said. She hit the disconnect button, took a deep breath, and managed a louder yell.

A face popped into view on one side of the opening from the trail and another appeared on the opposite side. Marge stifled a nervous giggle. The two disembodied heads peered at her for a moment before one reconnected with its torso and walked as far as the log where Marge stood.

"Where's the body?" he asked, looking around.

Marge pointed. "Behind that bush," she said. Please, God, let there be a body, she thought. Not just a hand.

Instead of walking in the direction Marge indicated, the policeman helped her move on legs that seemed to have lost their ability to function, guiding her back to the walking path. As she emerged from the woods, she saw the broad-shouldered form of Detective Pete Peterson reach the top of the wooden steps that were built into the trail.

An unexpected wave of relief warmed her, followed by confusion. Of all the emotions Detective Peterson had evoked in her a year ago, relief was not one of them.

Two more officers approached from the opposite direction. Detective Peterson stopped them with a movement of his hand. Brushing back a shock of gray-streaked brown hair from his forehead, he looked up and down and to either side of the trail, jotting in his notebook as he did so.

"Looks like this trail's too well used for any clues to surface," he said. "Check it out anyway though, just in case. Now, let's see where the body is." He started down the steps, glancing toward Marge, who was flanked by the first two police officers. His charcoal eyes widened in recognition. His strong square face reflected surprise and . . . something Marge couldn't decipher . . . then moved on as if she weren't there. At a light touch on her arm, Marge moved aside with the police officers so Detective Peterson had access to the opening.

He stood for a few minutes before inching down the hill. His eyes swept the ground in front of him as he made his way as far as the log. Marge congratulated herself for retracing her footsteps up to her backpack when she noted that the detective was also careful to walk in them. Squatting, he lifted the bent bush with his pencil, much as Marge had done earlier. After a long look, he stepped back and directed an officer with a camera to take photos from various angles.

A short heavyset man in a rumpled suit huffed slightly as he approached from the parking lot, carrying a medical bag. The focal point shifted to him as Detective Peterson stepped back; but the photographer stayed in place, moving closer and taking his direction from the new arrival.

"What are you doing here?"

Marge had been so intent on the unfolding events she hadn't seen Detective Peterson approach. He stepped in front of her, blocking her view.

"I came to do some drawing," Marge answered, embarrassed to hear the tiny sound of her voice. She took a deep breath and tried again. "I sat over there." She stepped to the side to see around him and pointed to the log. "When I looked closely at the brush, I saw those branches twisted in the wrong direction. I thought some animal must have clawed them, so I went to investigate. That's when I saw something blue. I started to lift the branch with my pencil when I . . . when I . . . saw it."

Detective Peterson watched Marge with narrowed eyes. "Can we get a blanket over here?" he yelled. Marge blinked in surprise to discover any warmth she felt earlier had departed, leaving her with a shiver she couldn't control. A young officer ran toward the parking lot. "Then what did you do?" The detective's voice seemed to echo through her thoughts. Marge was dismayed to feel herself sway. Taking off his jacket, Detective Peterson draped it over her shoulders. His unexpected chivalry nearly undid her. She bit back tears and pulled the jacket tighter, finding strength in its warm musky smell.

"I'm afraid I got sick first," Marge said. "After that I moved back as carefully as I could."

"Unfortunate but understandable," the detective said. "Discovering dead bodies is not something that gets easier with practice."

"So . . . it *is* a body? Not just a hand?"

Detective Peterson's dark-gray eyes narrowed again as he shot her a measuring look. "Why would you think it was just a hand?" he asked.

"That's all I saw. It looked so strange . . . out of place. Once I saw it, I couldn't look any further, so all I have in my mind is this hand with a denim cuff coming out of the earth, like it was planted there." She shuddered again and wrapped the detective's jacket closer.

"I remember you have a good eye for detail. Did you notice anything else?"

Marge hesitated. "It's probably nothing. I thought I heard a rustling in the bushes off to the left of the body." She pointed. "Maybe I frightened a small animal."

The detective immediately dispatched an officer to check out the area Marge had indicated.

It took Marge a moment to register that Detective Peterson had paid her a compliment. A resulting glow started to warm her but quickly dissipated when she tried to see what was happening around the body and realized he was again blocking her view. Deliberately, she thought. She didn't need his protection. She moved slightly so that she could see what was going on.

The photographer was still snapping pictures. Two other officers, under the direction of the man with the bag, were slowly and carefully removing the dirt covering the body, placing it as close to the victim as possible. Marge gulped and turned away, afraid she was going to be sick again, but she'd only had a cup of coffee in the morning so there was nothing more in her stomach to lose.

"Here, sit down," Detective Peterson said. He led her back to the wooden steps and laid the blanket the officer had brought on a step for her to sit on. He left Marge there, with his jacket still clutched around her.

Marge watched from a distance as the young officer Detective Peterson had sent into the bushes handed him something in a plastic bag. The detective then sent the officer and the photographer back into the brush.

What seemed to Marge like hours passed before the officers trudged up the steps, carrying the body in plastic wrap to a waiting gurney. Clouds now hid the sunlight that had tempted her out into the park so early in April. The late afternoon air was cooling fast.

"Anything you can tell me yet?" Marge heard Detective Peterson ask the man with the bag. At the same time, the detective glanced at Marge and steered the man, who she supposed was the medical examiner, out of earshot. Marge looked around. Detective Peterson had sent the other officers off on various missions, so no one was nearby to see her stand up and creep behind a large tree in order to hear.

"Not much," the medical examiner answered. "The victim was a young man, late twenties or early thirties. He was struck hard on the side of the head with an object that had a sharp edge. My guess is he was placed in the grave immediately after death occurred. The lividity is consistent with his position, so the hole was either dug very quickly or prepared ahead of time. The wound is consistent with a blow inflicted with the edge of a shovel and there appears to be blood mixed with the dirt that's over the body. If you happen to find a shovel in the vicinity, that would help. Rigor indicates he's been dead at least twelve and not more than twenty-four hours. I'll narrow that down for you as soon as I can."

"I wonder why the hand was sticking out?" the detective mused.

"Maybe the killer was in a hurry, careless, or . . ." The medical examiner paused. "While everything indicates the victim was dead before he was buried, I'll need to check what he aspirated to be absolutely certain."

Marge clutched her arms around her stomach to quell the dry heaves that threatened. She heard Detective Peterson spit out one word in a voice harder than she had ever heard during his investigation of Gene's death.

"Deliberate?"

"I don't know. It could just as well be that he was dead and the killer did a sloppy job of burying him. The only thing I'll go out on a limb for at this point is that you're either looking for an amateur or someone with a warped sense of humor. Or both."

The medical examiner turned to leave and Marge scurried back to the step. "Or someone with a warped sense of humor" echoed in her mind. She suddenly remembered the giggling she had dismissed as wind in the trees. She should tell Detective Peterson. Or would he give her that look, the one he so often gave her last year when he decided her ideas were too fanciful for consideration in an official investigation? After all, the man had been dead at least twelve hours. Why would anyone wait around that long?

But the officer *had* found something in the woods. She would tell the detective about the giggle after he finished with the medical examiner.

Marge tried to put an innocent look on her face when Detective Peterson returned. He eyed her with suspicion before helping her to her feet. "Don't say a word to anyone. I repeat, *anyone* . . . about how you found the body, especially about the hand sticking out of the ground. The more the public knows about this type of crime, the more kooks we'll have coming out of the woodwork claiming to have done it."

He handed Marge the backpack he must have retrieved after the photographer and medical examiner were finished. "I didn't see a car in the parking lot," he said. "Did you park nearby?"

Marge shook her head. "I walked."

Detective Peterson gave her a startled look. "From Newport Hills?" he asked. "Do you do a lot of that? I thought you had lost some weight."

Marge frowned at the rise of heat the compliment brought. She knew it turned her face red, accentuating the freckles that came with her fair skin. "I had to sell the house, remember? I moved into an apartment on Kelsey Ridge. But I do walk a lot—and exercise and take self-defense classes, too."

The detective nodded. "Still it's a fair distance," he said. "And self-defense classes are always a good idea."

Was that a glint of admiration Marge saw in his eyes? Before she could bask in it, he turned away and called an officer over, giving him instructions to drive her home. "Get someone to come and stay with you," he instructed. He seemed to notice for the first time that he held her sketchpad in his hand. He tore off the top sheet before handing it to Marge. "I'd like to keep this drawing for now," he said. "When you can face it, draw the scene before and after you saw the hand. Try to think if you saw or heard anything else unusual or if you saw anyone on or around the trail who might have seen something." Piercing eyes squelched any response she might have made. "Kelsey Ridge, huh? Sounds like you must have recovered your money."

The hint of derision in his voice brought Marge up straight. She searched for an appropriately cutting reply, but all she managed was, "I work hard to pay my rent."

"Don't tell me you stopped trying to get your money back. I thought you never gave up," he retorted as if unaware of her discomfort. He turned away and strode to the crime scene before she could think of an answer.

Marge felt tears prick. She shook them off. Why should she care what this detective thought of her? It wasn't for lack of trying that she hadn't recovered the money that had disappeared with Gene's death. Her daughter, Kate, an attorney, had helped Marge trace the money to an account in Switzerland. But by then it had been removed. The only money recovered, and shared among several people defrauded over the years, was from the sale of possessions left behind. Between that and the sale of her own house, Marge boasted a nest egg of nearly $250,000; less than half of what she had lost. Still, it was a nice cushion against poverty and a good sum with which to start rebuilding her retirement funds. Now all she had to do was manage not to spend it before she could accomplish the rebuilding and get to a retirement that was still fifteen to twenty years away.

Marge's anger dissipated during the walk to the parking lot, which seemed longer than when she had entered the woods earlier. The trees, which had been so inviting, now loomed over her; their dark shadows felt threatening. Her legs were unsteady, making her grateful for the officer's hand under her elbow. He was stone-faced and silent as he taxied her home and helped her out of the car. Marge half expected to see him salute before he drove off.

She trudged up the three flights of stairs, entered her apartment, and locked the door. Gazing around, she let the familiarity of the furniture she had retained from her family home relax her; the rocking chair, the one love seat that fit in the apartment from the pair that had been in the house, the small wooden kitchen table and chairs that had been the scene of family meals for so many years.

She dropped her backpack in the second bedroom and headed for the bathroom before she realized she still wore Detective Peterson's jacket. She pulled it close around her once more as she returned to the dining area. Taking it off, she ran her fingers across the shoulders after draping it over the back of a chair. He would be coming for that, as well as the picture.

She brushed her teeth, gargled, stripped, and stepped

into a warm shower. *Why a hand? Why sticking out of the ground? Why in Kelsey Creek Park?* The vision would not wash away. Her body would not get warm.

Pulling a brush through her unruly mop of auburn curls, she stared at her reflection in the mirror. The green eyes still carried a startled expression; the freckles stood out on her pale skin. She thought about calling someone for comfort, as Pete Peterson had suggested, but she had no desire to intensify the horror of the discovery by sharing it with someone else.

Slipping into her flannel nightgown and soft robe, she opened the bottle of Merlot Kate had brought the last time she joined Marge for dinner, grabbed a glass, sat in a darkening living room, and took a sip, waiting for it to soothe her. Wine was a luxury she could rarely afford, so it was a shame not to enjoy every sip. Unfortunately, this time it only upset her empty stomach and brought back bittersweet memories of the days when Gene took pride in supplying her with good wine.

Tears and a flash of resentment engulfed Marge. She thought she was long past this. She was supposed to forgive, right? After all, Gene was going to die before turning fifty, according to the doctor. But forgiveness was hard to come by when it cost Gene those last weeks of his life. Time he could have spent with his children. With her.

The man in the park was much younger. Did he leave a wife who would have to learn how to live without him, children who would grow up without their father? At least Kate and Robert were adults when Gene died. He had been there for their growing years and they had their memories.

After a couple more sips of wine Marge decided that drinking wasn't going to help answer any of her questions or make her feel better. Her stomach was still queasy and she knew she should eat something. She had missed lunch today, and the coffee she drank that morning had long ago been lost in the woods.

After putting together a tomato and cheese sandwich and taking the first bite, she discovered she was too hungry to remain squeamish for long. She flipped on the cassette player and sat in her rocking chair. Chewing each bite slowly, head back and eyes closed, she tried to concentrate on the magical piano of Karen Eikenberry's *Nightschool* and keep the day's events at bay.

It worked for about two minutes, then her head was invaded with worries about where her next temporary job would come from, how a forty-eight-year-old widow with a rusty applied-arts degree could find work that would pay the bills, whether she could do anything productive with her painting, whether Robert could salvage his marriage, and whether her friend Lori's husband was having another affair.

Finishing the sandwich, Marge corked the bottle of Merlot and took the half-full glass with her to the studio she had rigged up in the second bedroom. She would have to relive the horror, get it on paper. Maybe that would allow her to forget about it enough to sleep tonight.

When she had first moved into the apartment, she thought the smaller bedroom would make a wonderfully spacious studio where she could paint and teach art classes. Now, it was overflowing. In a corner near the window were an easel and a couple of her latest efforts: a portrait of Janette Jones, a stunningly beautiful African-American woman she had befriended at her current job; and a painting of the northern tip of Lake Washington framed by trees, which was the view from Robert's condo deck. The closet was full of supplies and additional artistic endeavors.

In another corner were four smaller easels and the equipment she used on most Sunday afternoons to teach art to four neighborhood girls. Marge smiled at the busyness of it. The room made her feel like a working artist.

Tomorrow afternoon, thank goodness, a birthday party for a mutual friend would keep all four of her students from their art class. She didn't think she could handle having them here this weekend.

She sat down at the easel, elected to forego watercolor pencils and went directly to paints. She closed her eyes. Why had she stepped off the hiking trail at that particular spot? What twist of fate dictated that she should be the one to slide through that narrow opening into the woods?

It had looked like the perfect place to draw, that's why. Easing past brambles and making her way down the slope and a few yards in from the trail, she had reached a fallen log that seemed to beckon to her. She smiled with the joy of being there, doing that. For too many years she had been content to be a good wife and mother. Now that the children were grown and Gene was gone, she could indulge herself. A familiar stab of guilt assailed her. Because Gene was gone, she could pursue her own interests. Did that mean she was glad he was dead?

Opening her eyes before she could get bogged down in that thought, she let the paintbrush take over. She started with the untamed ferns, the budding bushes, the sodden leaves on the ground . . . a large bush in front with new green buds stood out from the others. She pulled in a gnarled tree trunk that was in the near background and cocked her head, remembering. The brambles between the bush and the tree trunk shot out at angles and separated in an awkward pattern. She remembered thinking nature had to have a reason to be awkward.

Three hours later Marge heaved a sigh of relief. Working on automatic, she had completed two paintings. She turned away from them as soon as they were finished. If she didn't look at them again, maybe she could banish the vision of the hand.

As if it would be that easy to forget.

After cleaning up the paints, she thought she might follow Detective Peterson's suggestion and talk to someone. Maybe he was right—she needed to do that to purge the images. She glanced at her watch. Too late. Anyone she might phone would either be in bed or out on a Saturday night. She turned off the light in her studio, went into the bathroom to brush her teeth again, and finally crawled under the covers, convinced despite her weariness that she faced a night of insomnia.

MARGE AWOKE Sunday morning feeling refreshed. She must have fallen asleep as soon as her head hit the pillow. She lay in bed a few minutes, lulled by a light patter of rain that had begun sometime during the night and beat a tattoo into her dreamless sleep. As she lay there, the previous day's dark discovery crept back into her consciousness. She sat up in bed and tried on a smile to greet the day. To her surprise, it worked.

She showered and searched in her closet for something to wear to church. It was time to do some taking-in on her clothes; exercise and a change in eating habits had helped her shed over twenty pounds in the last year. She owned only a few clothes from her younger days that suited a woman her age and were the right size—but there was no room in her budget for a new wardrobe.

After pouring her first cup of coffee, Marge turned on the radio and listened to the news to hear what was being said about the body. It turned out to be very little. A body had been found in Kelsey Creek Park. According to the driver's license found in his wallet, and verified by his family, the victim's name was Luke Roddeman. The police had no comment on cause of death or how the body was found.

The last statements brought Marge fully awake. How had the press discovered the victim's name so soon? She hoped the police would never have any comment about how the body was found. She didn't need reporters camping on her doorstep, as they had when Gene supposedly committed suicide. After all, she had only found this body. She had no personal connection to the murder. Pete Peterson could solve this one without her help.

CHAPTER 2

THE PHONE RANG. "Marge?" Marge's first thought was that Lori was going to cancel their plans to spend time studying stocks for investment this afternoon. But there was a shrillness in Lori's voice that was unlike her usual calm.

"Lori, what's wrong?"

"You know that Luke Roddeman they found in Kelsey Creek Park?"

An uneasy feeling crept through Marge. "Yes," she managed.

"I was looking at Frank's schedule this morning and his name is on it. It looks like Frank had an appointment with Roddeman at eight o'clock Friday night."

"I'll be there in twenty minutes."

Marge glanced at the clock as she rushed to get ready. If she got to Lori's right away, she could still make the second service at church. She hesitated. She should tell her kids before the press discovered her name and spread it all over the airwaves, but Kate would still be in bed. Like her father, Kate's engine ran at full speed all week. She put in many extra hours at the corporate law office she had joined last year right out of law school. She compensated by playing hard Saturday night and sleeping away half of Sunday. She would not welcome a call at eight o'clock Sunday morning.

Marge bit her lip and scowled at the phone. Her daughter-in-law, Caroline, was sure to be up, but Marge had trouble making herself call Caroline. For the past year she had tried to stop avoiding Caroline, tried to appreciate her daughter-in-law's strengths and ambition, and tried to communicate with Caroline instead of always with Robert. Her efforts had resulted in a lowering of open animosity, but Marge always felt criticism lurking below the surface, as if Marge's having chosen to be a stay-at-home mom were responsible for all of the problems in Caroline and Robert's marriage.

Marge shook her head. She didn't have time to talk with Caroline.

Would she have made time for Kate?

Fifteen minutes later she pulled into Lori's driveway and stepped out of the car. Breathing deeply of the damp spring air to clear her thoughts, she turned and gazed across the street at the house that had been her home for twenty-two years. It looked different, even though she couldn't see that the new owners had done anything to make it so. It didn't look like home anymore. She wasn't even sure she knew the Marge Christensen who had lived there.

"Are you going to stand there gawking forever?" Lori's voice called out.

The unpredictable skies opened once more as Marge hurried into the house.

"I don't understand this," Lori said as soon as Marge was in the door. She marched into the kitchen, opened a cabinet, and grabbed two mugs as if on auto-pilot. "Frank isn't even in town. He has been on a business trip to Salt Lake City since last week. Why would that man's name be on his calendar?" She reached over and clicked off the screen saver, then turned back to pour coffee into the mugs. "I've been watching updates on TV since I talked to you. They've shown pictures of the man. He works in banking in some capacity—they said something I didn't catch about the main branch of our bank. He was only in his thirties."

Marge leaned down to look at the computer Lori kept on her kitchen desk. Lori had Frank's calendar open. There was a listing for each hotel where Frank would be staying, along with the phone number. Luke Roddeman's name was entered into Frank's calendar for Friday evening at eight o'clock. The night before Marge found the body. She stared at the screen, unable to move. That was within the twelve to twenty-four hours the medical examiner said the body had been dead. How did Frank know Luke Roddeman? And how could he have been meeting with Luke Roddeman if he was in Salt Lake City?

"I wasn't aware Frank knew the man," Lori said, her voice sounding as robotic as her actions. "I think I should call him. I should have done that already. He will probably want to hear about Roddeman's death." She set the mugs of coffee on the table with a thump and picked up the phone. Frank wasn't in the hotel, so Lori left a message for him to call when he got in.

Lori hung up and looked at Marge, a strange, quizzical

expression in her eyes. "Doesn't this remind you of that other time?" she asked, her voice tight. "When you asked me to call Frank and he was gone. That's when I found out he was having the first affair."

Marge stood, turned to Lori, and swallowed hard. It was tempting to try to put a wedge between Frank and Lori, to get Frank out of Lori's life so he couldn't hurt her anymore, but she couldn't let her friend start down this path for no reason. "Now, Lori, what would Frank do in the hotel room all day on a Sunday? Of course he's out, visiting, sightseeing, or taking care of business. That time, he was gone from the hotel the *whole* weekend without you knowing where he was."

"But you asked me to call him because it looked like there was a connection between him and what happened to Gene. Now it looks like there is a connection between Frank and this man that was killed in the park."

"Frank had nothing to do with Gene's death. They both happened to buy stocks from the same person, that's all. This connection, I'm sure, is just as innocent. But, Lori, why would he have an appointment for Friday when he was away on a business trip?"

Lori sank into a chair. "I don't know. He probably made the appointment and either forgot about it or cancelled it when he realized he would be away, but left it on the schedule." She looked up at Marge. "The police don't have to know about this, do they? You don't have to tell your Detective Peterson?"

Marge squirmed. "He's not my detective." She frowned, torn. "I don't know. If there is an innocent connection and we hide it, it will look bad if it comes to light." She didn't add that if the connection weren't innocent, they would be guilty of withholding evidence. She was almost as sure as

Lori that Frank couldn't have anything to do with murder. "You didn't happen to call Frank on Friday night, did you?"

Lori thought for a minute. Her face brightened. "Yes, as a matter of fact, I did. Brian came over and wanted to talk to his dad about something, so I called. Frank was out but called back within half an hour and talked to Brian. See, that proves he had nothing to do with the murder, so there is no reason to involve him with this, right? After all, hundreds of people probably know this man, Roddeman. Frank might have his name in the calendar to call him, or for some other reason altogether."

Marge hesitated. Even though it still angered her when she remembered how unresponsive the police had been while investigating Gene's death, she knew it was because they were convinced he had committed suicide. That's why whenever she discovered another piece of evidence she gave it to Detective Peterson. Those clues finally convinced him to reopen the case and eventually led them to Gene's killer.

"This is all the more reason to tell the police, Lori. Frank's time is covered, so they won't have any reason to suspect him. But they will know a little more about Roddeman's routine."

Lori frowned and turned away. Marge stood for a moment, caught in indecision. She knew she was right, but she feared that pressing the point could put their friendship on the line.

"Um, Lori, there is something else you should know." She could only hope Detective Peterson wouldn't object to her telling one of her two best friends at least this much.

It seemed to take an effort for Lori to look at her.

"I found Luke Roddeman's body."

Lori's brown eyes rounded in shock. "You're kidding! How did that happen?"

"It was such a nice day yesterday; I walked to the park to draw. I saw something strange about the bushes and went to investigate. I can't say much more about it. I don't know a whole lot more, and what I do know Detective Peterson has asked me not to tell."

"How awful. That must have brought back some painful memories."

"Yes," Marge said, not wanting to go down that avenue. "But I think I'm past that." She hesitated. "How are things between you and Frank?" she asked.

"We're doing fine. We're back in counseling and it looks like he's going to stick it out. He is so contrite over cheating after promising me it would never happen again. This time I think he really means it." Lori paused a moment. "At least, I try to convince myself he does. But it doesn't keep me from checking up on him every chance I get. He knows it's hard for me to learn to trust him again, so he makes sure I have all the phone numbers where he'll be staying and that's why he keeps his calendar where I can access it any time. Marge, please. You can't go to the police with this. Frank could not have murdered that man."

Silence stretched to an uncomfortable length.

"Marge?"

"Yes?"

"Could you show me where it happened?"

Marge stared at Lori. "What possible good could that do?" she asked. "You said Frank couldn't have been there."

"I don't know. I just need to see where it happened."

"Really, Lori, I've been there and there is nothing to see since the police have taken away the body. They searched the area thoroughly."

Lori was normally a calm, logical person, but when she dug in about something she was as bullheaded as they come. One look told Marge that was the case now. Besides, Lori had gone along with her own harebrained schemes when she was looking into Gene's death, so she didn't see how she could say no.

"I want to get to church at eleven o'clock," she said. "We'll need to take two cars."

Marge led the way to the park in her Honda, Lori following. When they reached the clearing where Marge had found the body, there was, as Marge had predicted, nothing to see. The police had even removed the yellow tape marking a crime scene, making it obvious nothing more was to be found. Even so, Lori stood at the opening to the clearing for a long time.

Marge looked off to the left when a rustling in the trees distracted her, remarkably like the noise she had heard yesterday.

"Marge?"

She scowled, the rustling leaving her uneasy. "Yes?"

"He was here."

"What?"

"He was here. Frank was here."

Marge looked over to see Lori pointing at a gold pen laying on the ground. Where did that come from? It wasn't there when the police investigated yesterday, Marge was sure of it.

"Lori, are you sure that's Frank's? Wait," she added, reaching out to stop Lori from going any closer. "Don't touch it. It's evidence."

"Do you think I'm going to leave it for the police? Frank didn't kill that man. He couldn't have. You have to help me prove it."

"We can't contaminate evidence, Lori. Please. That isn't the way."

But Lori wrenched away from Marge's grasp, grabbed the pen, and marched back to her car.

"You just go on to church," she said. "I'll manage without you."

Marge hesitated. She should tell the police, even though it would look worse now that Lori had taken the pen. But, if Lori wasn't going to listen to her, why should she get involved at all? Let them sort it out. She drove to church slowly, through raindrops that refused to stay away, even as the sun peeked from behind a low-hanging cloud.

Pulling through the circular drive into the parking lot, Marge groaned when she saw clutches of people standing around in front of the church, umbrellas coming down as the rain stopped. Usually they headed straight in, saving their conversation for coffee hour after the service. She could guess what made them change their pattern today—exactly what she was hoping the serenity of the church and the quiet of worship would wipe from her mind.

She groaned again and tried to get her responses in order when Millie Thompson, the church matchmaker and general busybody, came hurrying towards her. Marge's halfhearted smile was frozen on her face as she stood with her hand outstretched and Millie sailed past.

"Hello! You're new to our congregation. Welcome. Are you visiting the area or looking for a church home?"

Nothing like getting right to the point, Marge thought as she glanced back to see Millie greeting a tall, sandy-haired man who must have driven in right behind Marge. That answered one question Marge always had. Single men did, indeed, appear at the doorway of the church ready to have Millie put their lives in order. But she was also convinced Millie found some of them in the grocery store and extolled the virtues of the single female members of the congregation to get them to come to church.

Not one to let an opportunity slip by, as soon as Millie had determined the man's name, the fact that he was alone, and his intent to attend the service, she took him by the arm and hurried back to Marge. "Marge, I want you to meet Kevin Lewis. Kevin is visiting our church for the first time. I know you'll help him feel welcome." She turned twinkling eyes to Kevin. "Kevin, Marge was widowed last year and is an active member of our church. I'm sure she'll be glad to show you around."

Marge felt her face warm and cringed with the knowledge she was blushing. Did Millie have to be so obvious? After all, Marge wasn't looking for companionship. Before she could say anything, Millie scurried away to a group nearby, "My dear, did you hear . . ." trailing after her.

Marge turned to Kevin and swallowed the words of greeting that had started to form. The gleam in his light-blue eyes made the heat in her face travel down her neck. She managed to establish that he appeared youthful, surely younger than her forty-eight years. He was tall, lean, and tense—the picture of the beanpole her father often called her in her fast-growing years. Maybe because he was so wiry he appeared younger than he was.

Was she hoping? Was companionship perhaps a good thing?

His eyes continued to stare into hers. She had to force herself to turn away. She took a step back, her stomach fluttering. None of the other men Millie had thrown at her in the last year had had that effect.

"I think I might like this church," he said, his voice

coming out soft and clear. "It's not everywhere I go that I get introduced to the most attractive woman around as soon as I show up."

"Once Millie spots you, you'd better watch out or you'll find yourself married next week," Marge said as she started toward the church entrance. She jerked to a stop. Kevin, keeping pace behind, plowed into her and grabbed her arms to keep her from falling. Marge shut her eyes tight, trying to hide the quivers that radiated from Kevin's touch and wishing the words back into her mouth. What kind of an idiot blurted out the "M" word the first time she spoke to a man?

She was saved from further conversation when Millie hurried back, Lydia and Ron in tow. "Did you hear about the murder, Marge? Right here in Bellevue? I can hardly believe it," she chattered.

"What have you heard?" Marge asked cautiously, Kevin and his strange effect on her forgotten.

"Not much. Just that they found the body in Kelsey Creek Park." Millie looked as happily frightened as a child entering a haunted house on Halloween. "Buried," she whispered before she scurried off to make sure everyone else had heard the news.

"I wonder who found the body."

Marge started. Her stomach fluttered when she turned to face Kevin's penetrating gaze.

"It couldn't have been a pleasant experience," he added.

"I'm sure not," Marge agreed. No, not pleasant at all, she added to herself, and then hurried in to take her seat. Kevin slid into the pew beside her. The disconcerting feelings his nearness provoked made her miss the Prelude altogether.

It wasn't that she didn't recognize the sensation. After

all, she had been young once and was married for twenty-seven years. But she hadn't felt this way for a long time, much longer than the year Gene had been gone. She hadn't expected to ever again feel this kind of excitement, anticipation . . . fear.

"Given the tragic discovery in Kelsey Creek Park yesterday, we find ourselves asking why. Why did God allow a young man to be struck down; a young man who can't yet have had a chance to fulfill the promise of his life?" Marge's head snapped up.

"As God's people, we can be assured of His presence even when we cannot find the answers."

Marge blinked. Something inside her searched for more than the pastor's words gave her. Even though it didn't track with the loving God she thought she knew, a numbing fear had invaded her when Gene died. It was somehow her fault. In seeking a life of her own she had destroyed his.

"There are mysteries in life we are incapable of discerning, and evil we attempt to deny. We must only accept God is sovereign over all; ultimately He will prevail."

Marge was still deep in thought when Kevin reached over to turn her hymnbook to the song the rest of the congregation was singing. Her arm tingled where Kevin's had brushed against it.

"May I treat you to a cup of coffee?" he asked with a crooked grin after the Benediction, heading toward the gathering area where coffee and cookies were being served.

"Not today, thanks," she said. "But you should go ahead and meet some of the other church members." He followed her to the doorway.

"Don't forget Bible study Wednesday night," Millie sang out.

"Do I have to wait until Wednesday night to see you again?" Kevin asked. "What are you doing tomorrow?"

Marge's head swam. No, for this she wasn't ready. She might never be ready to get back on this particular roller coaster. Fortunately, this time, she had an out. "I do work, and I have an investment club meeting tomorrow night. So, are you coming to the Bible study on Wednesday?"

"Yes, I think I will. Until Wednesday."

Marge turned and almost ran down the steps. She breathed a sigh of relief as she drove out of the parking lot.

She was hardly in the door of her apartment when the telephone rang. "Marge, weren't you going to paint at Kelsey Creek Park yesterday?" Melissa's voice asked. Marge smiled. She should have known Melissa would make the connection right away.

"Yes, and I did," she said and waited for Melissa to follow up.

"Isn't that where that man was found dead?"

"Yes."

"Tell me you aren't connected with the discovery," Melissa said.

"I can't," Marge replied. "I found the body."

"I'm almost at your apartment. Five minutes tops," Melissa declared.

After listing and selling Marge's house in the aftermath of Gene's death, Melissa Horton had become Marge's other best friend. Melissa also helped her find this apartment and convinced her to pay a little extra rent for a place with an open view and closeness to the park. These amenities made all the difference in Marge's ability to adjust from a family house to a two-bedroom apartment.

"I hope you're not going to be making a habit of this,"

Melissa stated with characteristic abruptness when she strode in, her blue eyes crinkled in greeting.

"A habit of what?" Marge asked.

"Getting involved with police investigations."

"This is different," Marge protested. "I just found a body. I don't have any other involvement." It would be difficult to say anything more without mentioning Frank and Lori, and that she couldn't do.

"Uh huh," Melissa said, flipping her shoulder-length, slightly mussed blonde hair as she turned to go into the bathroom. Passing the studio door, she paused and looked in. Her eyes rounded and her mouth dropped open.

"Marge! Is that what you saw? A hand sticking out of the ground?"

"Oh, no! You weren't supposed to see that," Marge cried. "I promised Detective Peterson I wouldn't tell anyone any details."

"Detective Peterson . . . hmmm. Well, he can hardly call this one suicide or accidental." Melissa scrutinized the painting. "I hope you don't have to solve this one for him, too."

"No, no," Marge protested again. "I'm not involved at all. I probably won't hear from him again unless he needs a more formal statement about how I found the body."

"Marge, this is a powerful piece of work," Melissa said. "I've never seen you do anything like it before."

"I certainly hope not," Marge replied.

"No, I don't mean the subject matter. I mean the painting. It is so strong . . . so stark."

"It's just real," Marge said. "That was what I saw. In order to get it out of my head, I had to paint it. That's all." Even with the quick glance she gave it, unwilling to really look, she knew that wasn't all. Great. Probably the best work she had ever done and it was so gruesome no one would ever want to hang it.

"Anyway," Marge continued, "don't tell anyone about it, or what the police know about how the man died, please. You'll get me in trouble with that detective again. And if word ever gets out that I found the body, I'll have reporters all over me again, too."

"Mum's the word," Melissa promised as she continued into the bathroom. "What a horrible thing to find in the park," she said as soon as she returned. She sat on the sofa, slipped out of the sandals she preferred to wear in all but the coldest weather, and tucked her feet up under her flowing Indian skirt. "You must have been in shock."

"It's strange," Marge said. "I couldn't get it out of my mind. I thought I'd never sleep again. Per Detective Peterson's instructions, I painted that picture. After finishing it, I went to bed and slept the sleep of the uninvolved."

"What a gift that is," Melissa exclaimed.

Marge squirmed, looking for a way to discourage more talk before she let something slip about Lori. Melissa seemed to pick up on her discomfort, because after a pause and a penetrating look she changed the subject. "How's work?"

"I'm afraid it's not going to last much longer," Marge replied. "We've almost completed coding for computer retrieval of all the documents that have been subpoenaed for the case. I don't see how it can be more than another week."

"That has to be one of the longest temporary jobs around," Melissa said.

Marge laughed. "Well, I heard document coding for the WPSS litigation in the eighties went on for several years. This one has only been about four months."

"So, what comes next?"

"I haven't been spending enough time looking for what comes next. My overtime work and Sunday art class have kept me busy."

"Marge, you have to get more serious about your finances. You're barely squeaking by and still using some of your savings. What if something happens to keep you out of work or no good assignment comes along for awhile? You'll eat up all your investment money."

Marge grinned, hiding her anxiety. "I still have a little money left over from selling Gene's BMW," she said. "So, the money from selling our house and the victim's settlement is in CDs and earning interest. It will do even better as I apply more of what we're learning and get it invested in something that will grow."

Still, she thought, Melissa was right. She had stretched the money from selling the BMW with income from temporary work about as far as it would go. She couldn't use the investment money for daily living. Not unless she planned on working for the rest of her life. If she used it to go back to school and get her certificate, she could make a decent living teaching classroom art, and she could probably teach long enough to get a small pension on top of Gene's social security. But her Sunday art class already consumed a lot of her creative energy. In the demanding position of a full-time teacher she could forget about having enough creativity left over for her own work.

Not again. Compromising was okay then, but this was now. Her family was grown, Gene was gone, and it was time to do what she wanted with her life. She only needed to figure out how to make a living at it.

"Did you get your stock study done for tomorrow night's investment club meeting?"

Marge grinned. Naturally, that would be the next subject, since it was one of the ways she, Melissa, and Lori were trying to grow their money. Lori, always the pragmatic one, had taken control of her own finances at the first whiff of trouble in her marriage. Melissa was an independent single woman, and appeared ready to stay that way, but whether she did or not she intended to provide for her own financial security. And Marge needed to grow back the retirement funds Gene had lost.

"No, Lori and I were thinking about doing that this afternoon, but my discovery chased it right out of my mind."

"Well, I hope Lori has done some work on it."

Marge hesitated.

"What?" Melissa asked. "Is there something that chased it out of Lori's mind, too?"

"No," Marge said, but couldn't make the unaccustomed lie convincing. As close as she was to both women, Marge didn't feel free to discuss Lori's business with Melissa. Especially not when it had to do with a murder. Although Melissa did know about Frank's affairs.

"Frank hasn't had another affair, has he? If so, she'd better drop him this time. She should have done it a long time ago."

"No, I'm sure not," Marge said, glad to be able to answer truthfully. "She couldn't reach him today, that's all. He'll call back, then there'll be no doubt."

"Really!" Melissa said. "I think I heard about something like that once before."

"Can you join me for lunch?" Marge asked, hoping to change the subject again.

Melissa stood. "No, I hate to run off so fast, but I have to get to an appointment. I just stopped by to check on you. Are you sure you're okay? This discovery of yours isn't going to haunt you?"

"I don't think so. I'll give you a call if I need someone to hold my hand," Marge said.

"Well, try to get some investment work done this afternoon. We need to make some decisions about what stocks to buy this month."

After Melissa left, Marge threw together a tuna fish sandwich and poured a glass of iced tea for her late lunch. Pulling on a sweater, she took her portable radio out to the deck to eat, to bask in what had turned into a sunny afternoon, and to smell the scents of early spring. She would not think about Frank and Lori.

Tomorrow it would be back to work. She had Kate to thank for the job. A friend of Kate's worked for a Seattle law firm that hired people practically off the street to read and code litigation documents for computer indexing. The short time frame for completing the documentation meant ten-hour days and some six-day weeks, so Marge had been enjoying a salary that more than paid her rent and groceries for the first time since she started temporary work.

Lori called shortly after Marge finished lunch.

"Frank called back," she said, her voice flat.

Marge felt muscles she hadn't realized were tense relax. Frank was where he said he would be. This time.

"He said Luke Roddeman called him about a dormant account he found at the main branch of First Bank in Seattle in Frank's mother's name. Evidently she had not told anyone or kept any record about the account so it wasn't included in the estate when she died. Frank didn't have time to talk, and told Roddeman he would be away this week. Once Roddeman verified that Frank was the heir to the money, he insisted on calling Frank at his hotel in Salt Lake City. He said it couldn't wait and insisted Frank put the time in his calendar so he wouldn't forget to be there. But he didn't call. That's all. Frank doesn't see any reason why the police have to be told. Nor do I."

Marge frowned. "Um, Lori, what time did you call Frank on Friday?"

"About seven o'clock. Why?"

"And what time did he call you back?"

"Seven-thirty. I remember because the TV program Brian was watching had just ended."

Marge sighed. "Good. He would have been at the hotel room in time to wait for Roddeman's call." Marge knew that Lori, armed with this new evidence that Frank was not involved with the murder, would expect her to stay quiet about Roddeman's name on his scheduler. "But, Lori, I'm sure the police are going to try to reconstruct Luke Roddeman's movements for some time leading up to his death. If Frank is on Luke's schedule, like Luke is on Frank's, the police are going to find out anyway. Don't you think it would be better to let them know up front?"

"Frank figured you would find some reason to go to the police," Lori said, anger sharpening her voice. "He said our friendship wouldn't be enough to stop you from getting involved."

"I don't intend to get involved, Lori, and it has nothing to do with our friendship." Marge couldn't hide her own anger and was sure Lori could hear it in her voice. She hated the idea that Frank, who by rights Lori should have kicked out long ago, dared to cast doubts on their friendship. "But, if we have some information the police might need, we should give it to them."

"Do what you have to do," Lori said and slammed down the phone.

Marge waited a few minutes to steady her breathing. Frank's comments did irritate her, but she couldn't make a decision based on anger. If she told the police, and that drew their suspicions to Frank, she would feel obligated to try and find the truth. But since Frank was in Salt Lake City, he couldn't be suspected, so she didn't need to get involved. In either case, if she didn't tell the police, both she and Lori would be guilty of impeding the investigation.

The same way Frank impeded the investigation of Gene's death when he wouldn't tell who handled the investments both the men had made. It had been the wrong decision, which delayed police action almost too long. It was not the right thing to do, then or now. She picked up the phone and called Detective Peterson before she lost her conviction.

"He's not available. May I take a message?"

"Please ask him to call Marge Christensen." She gave her phone number and hung up. She wondered if the detective took Sundays off when he had a murder investigation to conduct.

Fifteen minutes later the phone rang. Marge grabbed it, expecting to hear Detective Peterson's voice.

"Marge Christensen? This is Paula Manford from *The Seattle Times.* I understand you discovered the body in Kelsey Creek Park yesterday. Can you tell me how you happened to do that?"

CHAPTER 3

MARGE SLAMMED DOWN the receiver. Lori? Impossible. As upset as Lori was, Marge could not imagine she would contact the press. Would Frank do it, from Salt Lake City, out of spite? Surely not. More likely it was a leak from the police station. That happened all the time, didn't it?

The phone rang again. Marge raised the receiver, listened for a moment, and dropped it back into the cradle when another reporter identified himself. After three more calls from reporters she was ready to pull out her curly mop of hair.

Thankful that she hadn't discarded Gene's old office phone with its sophisticated answering capabilities, she went into the spare bedroom and rooted around until she found it. When she moved into the apartment, she had bought a new phone with a digital answering machine, figuring that would be cheaper than paying for voice mail every month and more reliable than the audiotape in Gene's machine. But the tape in the old answering machine was removable and the machine could be programmed to give a recorded message after one ring.

By the time she returned to the living room, the telephone was ringing again. Another reporter. After two more interruptions, Marge disconnected it from the jack and replaced it with the old equipment. She left it disconnected while she collected her thoughts, then she pressed the "record message" button.

"I have nothing to say to the press. If you are calling for another reason, please leave a message."

Once the system was in place she replaced the receiver and connected the phone to the jack. It rang immediately. She heard her message and the recording tape click on.

"What kind of game are you playing with the phone?" Detective Peterson's voice asked.

Marge grabbed the receiver. "Don't hang up Detective Peterson," she cried.

She heard a sigh at the other end of the line at the same time the tape clicked off. "Call me Pete, please," he said in a tired voice. It became businesslike when he repeated, "What is going on with your phone?"

"A few minutes ago I got a call from Paula Manford of *The Seattle Times.* She wanted to ask me about finding the body. After that the phone started ringing constantly—reporters looking for information—so while I hooked up Gene's old phone and answering machine I wasn't taking calls."

"How did the press find out?" the detective demanded.

"Perhaps I should be asking you that question," Marge shot back.

The line was silent.

"Detective Peterson?"

"I'd like to say it couldn't have come from here," he finally said. "If I find out it did, rest assured someone's head will roll. Is that what you called me about?"

"Oh, no," Marge said, suddenly realizing that he was returning her phone call. "You remember Lori and Frank Knowles? They used to be my neighbors across the street?"

"Of course. He's the one who withheld evidence that would have cleared up the loss of your savings days earlier, and maybe even your husband's murder."

Marge couldn't help the grin that spread across her face. No sympathy in that department. "Lori heard the name of the man found in the park, Luke Roddeman, on the news this morning. Later she saw his name on Frank's computer scheduler. Frank had an appointment with Luke Roddeman on Friday, even though Frank is away on a business trip."

"I suppose Frank Knowles is unreachable again."

Marge thought she knew the detective well enough that she could detect surprise if it was in his voice. There wasn't any. That worried her. "Well, he's still away; but this time Lori has the phone number of the hotel where he is staying. She already talked to him, and he says Roddeman was supposed to call him at his hotel about a dormant account his mother left when she died."

"I suppose your friend Lori suspects you were going to tell me about this and that she's okay with it?"

"Well . . . yes and no," Marge admitted.

"Don't you think she's a more likely source of your leak to the press than a trained and professional police department?"

"I can't believe that of Lori," Marge declared. She started to hang up before remembering to add, "By the way, I've completed the paintings you asked for. You can pick them up anytime. And your jacket, too."

Twenty minutes later Marge wanted to cover her ears. She felt a scream building in her throat. One ring, listen to her message, listen to the caller, another ring, repeat. Sometimes the person asked her to call back, more often they took the hint and hung up without leaving a message. One caller held onto the receiver a few moments before making a noise that sounded like a giggle. Marge frowned. It reminded her of the noise she heard in the park. She shook her head. She must have heard it wrong. Paula Manford called three times, urging Marge to tell what she knew so media reports would be accurate.

Marge tried to paint, but the constant ringing and message recording destroyed her concentration. She finally tossed aside her paintbrush and strode to the phone. "I know one good way to stop the ringing," she said aloud. "I'll keep the phone busy myself." She dialed the number for Kate's downtown Seattle apartment.

"Mother, what are you getting into?" Kate asked as soon as she answered the phone.

"What do you mean?" Marge asked, guilt sweeping over her. She had forgotten to call after her disagreement with Lori this morning. She should have warned both Kate and Robert before they heard it on the news. Since reporters were calling her, they had probably already made her name public.

"I've had reporters calling here asking what I know about the body you found in the park. Tell me it isn't true."

"I'm afraid it is. I don't know how the press discovered that I found it, or your connection to me, but I guess it's all over town by now."

Marge answered Kate's questions about how and where

she discovered the body, but left out the part about the burial and the hand. That finished the subject pretty quickly.

"I think I'd better hang up and call Robert," Marge said. "If the press found you this quickly, they must have found him, too. I'm sure Caroline is thrilled."

"Mom," Robert's voice boomed with unusual buoyancy when she greeted him. "I'm glad you called. I think we might have a little problem."

Marge pulled the receiver away from her ear and stared at it for a moment. The words didn't track with the tone of his voice, and remembering the rough time Robert and Caroline's marriage had gone through shortly after Gene's death made her worry. She wasn't sure it had ever recovered completely. "What problem?" she asked.

"People keep calling here to ask Mrs. Christensen about a body in the park. The first time someone asked for Mrs. Christensen, I gave the phone to Caroline and she was thoroughly confused. We finally figured out they wanted to talk with you."

Marge nearly laughed at herself for manufacturing problems and forgetting the one she had called about. "I'm afraid they do. Unfortunately, I found a body when I went to draw in the park yesterday. Somehow the press found out who discovered the body, so this afternoon I've been bombarded with calls. They also seem to have tracked down both you and Kate. I'm sorry."

"Sorry for what? Not that they're calling us, I hope. How else would I know that you've gotten yourself involved in police business again?"

Marge sat up straight. How could Robert be harping on that? If she hadn't involved herself in police business,

Gene's death would have remained on the books as a suicide and she would have recovered nothing of the money that had been swindled from them. "That's what I was calling to tell you about. And, I am not involved except for having discovered the body. I'm sure you're not suggesting I should have walked away and not told the police about it. Anyway, since you already know, I guess there is nothing more to say."

"Hold on, Mom." The different tone had returned to Robert's voice, keeping Marge from hanging up. "There's something I want to tell you, too. Um . . . uh . . . you're going to be a grandmother."

Marge nearly dropped the phone. "How did that happen?"

Robert chortled. "The usual way," he said.

"I thought Caroline insisted you use birth control."

"She did. We were double protecting as usual, since Caroline wouldn't hear of having a child and insisted I take precautions, then didn't trust me to do it so added her own. But something still seems to have gone wrong . . . or right," he added.

Marge had never allowed herself to consider what Caroline might do in the unlikely event she became pregnant. Even though Robert sounded pleased, she had to bite her tongue to keep from asking. As if reading her thoughts, Robert said, "She has agreed to have the baby as long as I take complete responsibility for it after it is born. Of course, I agreed."

My son, the house husband, Marge thought. What did he know about taking care of a baby?

"Hello, Marge," Caroline's clipped voice came on the line before Marge could digest the news. "I'm sure you're happy to know you're finally going to be a grandmother."

"Congratulations." Marge wondered if Caroline could hear the echoing going on between her ears.

Caroline laughed. "Congratulate Robert, not me. You thought I'd never do it, didn't you? Actually, I didn't. Not on purpose, that is. It was an accident. But Robert's been bugging me for a child, so I thought I might as well go ahead and have this one and get it over with."

Marge frowned. Would one caring parent be enough? Especially if the child lived in the same house with a parent who didn't care? Although, that might not be the case. Strange things happened to women when they bore children. Often ambivalent first timers, holding that tiny baby who was totally dependent on them, discovered a depth of love they never before knew existed.

"When is the baby due?" she asked.

"Early October. I plan to work as long as I can before taking maternity leave; and I will go back to work as soon as possible. I'm having my tubes tied right after giving birth so this can't happen again. It'll be up to Robert to take paternity leave or put the baby in day care."

Caroline's voice sounded defensive; Marge knew it was because she expected Marge to disapprove. Caroline made no secret of her disdain for what she considered Marge's old-fashioned views about life and marriage. She probably expected Marge to object to Caroline having her tubes tied as well as for leaving the baby in another's care. True, both were outside Marge's comfort zone; and true, she had been a stay-at-home wife and mother, but she never claimed her way was the only way.

If Caroline had her tubes tied immediately after the baby was born, would she have a chance to hold the baby first, perhaps feel it touch her heart? If she did, she might change her mind. Marge didn't plan to hold her breath, though.

"October?" She finally managed to say. "You're already over three months along?"

"Yes. Because we were being so careful, it took me awhile to wake up to the fact I had a problem; still longer to decide I should go to the doctor to find out what the problem was. What a surprise I had in store!"

Marge felt dizzy. "Well, congratulations, anyway," she managed. "Also, I apologize for the hassle you're getting about the man I found in the park."

Caroline had a *problem*, Marge thought, as she hung up the phone. She thought about when she discovered she was pregnant with Robert, long before she and Gene planned to have children. She couldn't remember ever thinking of her pregnancy as a *problem.*

She tried to shake her mind clear at the ring of the telephone. She didn't have time to worry about Robert and Caroline. It wasn't as if she could do anything about it. She had to put it in God's hands and trust Him to help them do the right thing.

Easier said than done.

When the recorder picked up the call, she heard Lori's voice, high-pitched and hysterical. She grabbed the receiver before Lori could hang up.

"I hope you're satisfied," Lori cried. "The police arrested Frank for murdering that man."

Marge gasped, unable to speak. "How could they do that? Or even think he did it? He's out of town."

Lori's sobs turned to anger. "No, he isn't out of town. Remember how I never got through to him directly? I left a message and he called me back? It turns out he was shacked up somewhere in Seattle, having his messages forwarded from Salt Lake City, and the police tracked him down."

Marge shook her head, hardly able to believe what she was hearing. Shacked up in Seattle? Forwarding calls from Salt Lake City? It didn't make sense.

"Are you there?" Lori's voice was strident.

"Lori, I'm so sorry . . ."

Lori didn't let Marge finish. "You're sorry! Why did you tell them? Now that they think they have the answer to the murder, do you think they will look any further? Did they with Gene? Frank might be an unfaithful husband, but he isn't a killer. You know that, as well as I do. So, what are you going to do to help me prove his innocence?"

"What?" Marge asked, sitting down.

"You got us into this. What are you going to do to get us out?" Lori demanded.

She sagged against the chair. "How did *I* get you into this? If Frank had been where he said he was, he wouldn't be under suspicion."

"You went to the police, didn't you? You couldn't stop from telling all to your precious detective. If you value our friendship, you will help me prove Frank didn't do it. You've known Frank for years. You know he couldn't kill anyone."

Marge thought she knew that—but she wouldn't have believed Frank would cheat on Lori either.

"Don't you think the police would have found out without me? In fact, Detective Peterson didn't sound at all surprised when I talked with him. I think they were already looking for Frank." She paused, suddenly overwhelmed by what Lori was asking her to do. "Lori, I have no idea where to begin to find any answers."

"Right," Lori said. "You didn't worry about where to begin when you investigated Gene's death. You just did it. And I recall accompanying you on one or two escapades. All I'm asking for is the same consideration."

Marge sighed. She knew she couldn't let Lori feel abandoned by her best friend. After all, it was true. Lori had helped Marge solve Gene's death. Taking a deep breath, she plunged in. "All right, I'll do what I can to help you, but I can't promise it will do any good. If we work together, we might be able to dig up something to point the police away from Frank. "By the way, Lori," she added, "did you call the press about my finding the body?"

That seemed to shock the anger out of Lori. "Of course not. I'd never do something like that to you. Not after what you went through when Gene died."

Marge relaxed a little. That sounded like the old Lori.

Her mind was already whirring, seeking a few pieces of the puzzle that might fit together. "When did Frank get back into town? Can you find out if he went to the office on Friday? And if not, where was he? And why was his business trip cut short?"

If it was. Marge couldn't help thinking.

"There's no way I can do that," Lori said. "Frank is furious with both of us. He won't tell me anything and he wants you to stay out of it; so we have to be careful what he might find out about."

"I don't have any authority to ask questions," Marge said, ignoring the remark about staying out of it. She didn't much care what Frank wanted, and she was sure that when Lori calmed down she would refuse to give in to his demands. "As Frank's wife, you should be able to convince his office you need the information."

"Don't you think the police would know by now?"

Marge thought a moment. "Probably. But if the police don't tell us, and Pete Peterson is not likely to tell me anything, we need to find out for ourselves what they know that implicates Frank."

"Frank's attorney is trying to get bail, so Frank should be out soon. I really don't think I can go to his office without him finding out. He's so angry I probably won't even be able to get in touch with you either, unless I kick him out again, and I don't believe in kicking a man when he's down."

Lori hung up before Marge could respond. Marge stared at the phone. Hadn't Lori asked her to help? And now she refused to try to get any information herself?

Maybe I should forget about it, she thought. Maybe it wouldn't be such a bad thing for Frank to be found guilty. If only her experience after Gene's death didn't lead her to agree with Lori that once the police were convinced they had a suspect they would put all their energies into building their case against that person instead of looking further. As much as Marge had learned to distrust Frank in the last year, as much as she wanted to believe the worst of him, she couldn't convince herself that he would kill anyone.

But who could imagine anyone they knew would kill someone?

Anyway, even if Lori would be better off without Frank, she wouldn't be better off with him in prison. If there was a chance he was innocent, they had to find it.

The phone rang again. Marge listened to her message and heard the recorder click on. "Mrs. Christensen, this is Paula Manford again. Please call me back. I'm only doing my job, trying to get the facts straight before printing my story. Is it true that you found the body because its hand was sticking out of the ground—that an attempt had been made to bury the body?"

Marge stared at the machine. Well, at least that answered one question. Lori wasn't the leak because Lori didn't know about the hand. The only possible source was the police department.

That gave her an excuse to call Detective Peterson again. And while she had him on the phone maybe she could find out what made them believe Frank was the killer. She picked up the phone and dialed the number.

"Pete Peterson here."

Marge was so startled at getting through directly to Detective Peterson rather than to someone asking her to leave a message, it took her a moment to find her voice. "This is Marge Christensen," she said when she could manage it. "I think you'd better start to look for that head to roll in the police department."

"What?"

"You said if the leak about my finding the body came from the police department someone's head would roll. Well, a reporter asked me about finding the body buried with its hand sticking out of the ground. I never told Lori that. It could only have come from the police department."

"Or the killer, if he wanted to make trouble for you."

Marge thought about that for a moment. "How would the killer know I discovered the body? I don't think it's been on the news yet. And what would he gain by making trouble for me? Besides, if Roddeman wasn't dead when he was buried, the killer probably thought he was. If Roddeman was trying to dig his way out, the killer wouldn't know anything about the hand sticking up."

She could almost hear the gears turning in Detective Peterson's head in the long silence that followed. "All right," he finally said, "it sounds like you heard a little more than you should have out there in the park. I guess

I'd better tell you the medical examiner determined that Roddeman was dead before he was buried. So, the killer knew and could have called the press himself. It doesn't matter anyway, because as soon as we tie up a few loose ends we'll give all the details to the press and they'll stop bugging you."

"What makes you think Frank Knowles would commit murder?" Marge asked quickly, before the detective could hang up.

Another silence. "Did I let that slip?" he asked.

"Lori called and told me," Marge said. "And that Frank was in a motel room in Seattle. She is furious with me for calling you in the first place."

"She should be furious with her husband. Why would he be with the dead man's girlfriend in a motel room in downtown Seattle?"

"That doesn't make him a killer," Marge blurted before the detective's words hit her. *With the dead man's girlfriend?* The police might have more of a case than she thought.

"The girlfriend seems to think it does." He paused. "Now I did slip. You didn't know it was Roddeman's girlfriend, did you?"

Marge felt an unaccountable urge to ease the detective's conscience. "Well, no; but Lori did say he was shacked up." She hurried on before he could cut her off. "So, with the possibility of discovery threatening, Frank went to the park with a shovel and took the time to dig a shallow grave and bury Roddeman after killing him? He did this on Friday night and was still at the park when I showed up Saturday afternoon, so that he could giggle at my discomfort? Then he called the press to make me even more uncomfortable?"

"Giggle?"

Marge could almost see the detective sit up straighter in his chair.

"You didn't tell me about any giggle."

"It slipped my mind because I was so upset . . . it was probably only wind in the trees," Marge explained. "Besides, what good does knowing about it do you?"

It wasn't gears turning that Marge heard in the silence this time. And when Detective Peterson spoke, there was sternness in his voice. "Mrs. Christensen, this is a police matter. I've said too much already because inadvertently you have become involved in the case. But you need to back off and leave the rest to the police."

Marge had one more thing to say before she would let the detective hang up. "Does it make any sense to you that a man who has had two affairs in a little over a year, and dropped them as soon as his wife found out, would suddenly become so enamored with a woman that he would kill for her? Besides, what about Frank's mother's dormant bank account? Isn't that a bit too much of a coincidence?"

Another short silence. Long enough to make Marge wonder if the police had paid any attention to the dormant bank account. But they had to look into every angle, didn't they? "That's it. No more. You paint your pictures and leave the police work to the police. That's an order, Marge Christensen. I will come by tomorrow afternoon to pick up those paintings. After that, I don't want to hear from you about this case again."

Marge stared at the phone for a long time after she hung up. Even though being given orders didn't sit well with her, she truly wanted to follow Pete Peterson's instructions. The circumstances were different—Frank certainly wasn't anything like Gene—but it hit too close to home, opened up old wounds. She couldn't let it go. For Lori's sake, she had to prevent Frank from going to prison for a crime he didn't commit. *If* he didn't commit it.

But, how did Frank's pen get to the crime scene?

On a sudden impulse, she picked up the phone and dialed the number Paula Manford had left.

"Mrs. Christensen," Paula said when Marge identified herself. "I'm so glad you called. When can we sit down and talk?"

"I don't have anything to add to what you already know, Ms. Manford," Marge said. "And even if I did, the police have sworn me to secrecy, which makes me wonder who has been handing out information to the press."

"You know I can't give up confidential sources. Although, in this case it doesn't matter, because I don't know who the source is. The information comes in muffled phone calls, which is why I've tried so hard to get to you to verify it before we go to print. This source is evidently calling every newsperson in the area, with the result that other reporters are scooping me. Since the source seems to be accurate and you won't answer any questions, I can't hold back any longer."

"Do you keep those phone calls on tape?" Marge asked.

"Why, yes, we do."

"Please make sure they aren't destroyed. The police might be able to make some use of them."

"Mrs. Christensen, this is not the first crime I have reported. I know when to contact the police and have already done so, thank you. If you don't have anything to add to the information we already have, I need to get a column out."

"I hope you do some checking yourself before labeling Frank Knowles a murderer," Marge said.

She could sense Paula's interest perk up. "What reason do you have for believing he is innocent?" she asked. "Do you know the suspect personally?"

Marge could have bitten her tongue. One day in the next millennium she might learn to think before she spoke. Paula might not even have known about Frank, but from her response Marge doubted it. "I don't have anything more to say," she said and hung up the receiver before the reporter could ask more questions.

What had that accomplished? As far as Marge could tell, the only thing she had proven was what Detective Peterson kept saying—she was an amateur and should leave the police work to the professionals.

Marge turned down the volume on the phone and answering machine as low as it would go. Putting her head back, she sat in her favorite chair, rocking gently, trying to make sense out of what was happening. It didn't work.

Unable to stay still, she picked up the sketchpad she kept on the table beside her. She frowned; she was too unsettled to think of something to draw. After a moment's hesitation, Marge let her fingers take the lead. Before she realized what was happening, a face had emerged. A head of unruly hair topping a square face with a strong jaw. A frowning brow over intense gray eyes. Mouth set in a firm line. Irritated, she tore off the sheet, balled it up, and tossed it in the trash.

That man was so sure of himself; but he had been wrong about Gene. She was certain he was wrong about Frank, too. What hope did she have of proving it?

Marge dropped the sketchpad on the table and slipped a low-impact aerobics tape into the VCR. She worked out for half an hour, trying to tire herself enough to fall asleep. A vigorous exercise might have worked better, but in a third-floor apartment jumping up and down was not a good idea, and she didn't feel up to a trip downstairs to the workout room.

The exercise, followed by a warm shower and a glass of the wine she had opened last night, did the trick. She slept soundly until aroused by the alarm the next morning.

CHAPTER 4

Marge's workplace on the tenth floor of a downtown Seattle high-rise was effectively sealed away from the ever-changing spring weather. In its sterile confines, she was sure she could forget about Saturday's events and concentrate on the task at hand.

She was wrong. For the third time she read the list of company directors from the 10-K form. For the third time she checked them against the coded entries on the computer input form she was reviewing. For the third time she had no idea if they matched.

She needed a break. Rising, she walked into the cubicle that served as the lunchroom. The coffeepot was empty, which was no surprise. Why would anyone think to start a fresh pot because they had finished the last of the previous one? While she was waiting for the coffee to brew, Janette Jones joined Marge in the cubicle.

"That'll teach you to take the whole weekend off,"

Janette said in her low throaty voice, careful not to disturb the coders on the other side of the partition.

Janette's perfect chocolate skin, large soft-brown eyes, and pronounced cheek and jaw lines, enhanced by hair pulled back into an old-fashioned chignon, made Marge want to grab a sketchpad and put her elusive beauty on paper. No matter how many drawings and paintings Marge had done, she always saw something in her friend that she had been unable to capture.

A good ten years younger than Marge, Janette was a singer and actress who worked in occasional plays and had won a few small roles in the movies increasingly being filmed in Seattle. She filled the time between roles singing in local jazz lounges and doing temporary jobs like this one.

"I suppose everyone here knows," Marge said.

"I arrived too late this morning to talk, the same as you. We'll find out at coffee break, I'm sure. In case I don't get a chance to talk to you again today, I'll see you at the investment club meeting tonight."

What was Janette talking about? They had lunch and two breaks together every day. Surely they'd see each other, as usual, for one or all of them.

After replenishing their mugs, they made their way back to their seats, joining the rows of heads studiously bent to the task of printing block letters into individual boxes on computer forms. The forms would be sent someplace offshore and the coded information entered into a computer database by keyers who probably had no idea what the shapes meant but had learned to type them on an English keyboard at over a hundred characters a minute.

How ironic it seemed to Marge that one of the main requirements for this job associated with the latest in computer technology was the ability to print neat block letters; a skill that was usually learned in kindergarten.

Normally at break time Janette and Marge took a short brisk walk. Today Marge didn't make it to the door.

"Was it really you who discovered the body?" someone asked in a tone of disbelief.

"What were you doing in the woods?" This voice was filled with intrigue.

"Didn't you read?" another asked. "She was painting. She's an artist. And we never knew."

"A hand sticking out of the ground! How gruesome!"

Marge looked around for Janette and saw her hovering in the background with a half smile and a teasing twinkle in her eyes. Groaning, Marge proceeded to tell the group everything she had already heard on the news. They seemed to savor it more coming from her lips.

"A love triangle. How romantic," one girl intoned.

Marge felt dizzy. Love triangle? Where did that come from?

"Since when is murder romantic?" asked another.

"So, do you think Frank Knowles was having an affair with this woman, like the papers are saying?" asked a third.

"No," Marge said, louder than she intended, silencing the room.

"No," she repeated in a lower voice. "I happen to know Frank Knowles, and he wouldn't be having an affair now."

"Now?" asked a sharp listener. "As opposed to some other time?"

Marge sighed. She supposed all this would come out in the news anyway. Besides, no one in this group knew Frank or Lori personally. "He is in marriage counseling right now, and his marriage is very important to him. He would not jeopardize it this way."

"So, who is Tracy Generas?"

"Who?" Marge asked.

"Tracy Generas. The last radio update I heard said Frank Knowles was in a motel room with Tracy Generas."

Good question, thought Marge when break was over and they returned to their seats. Who is this Tracy Generas? And what was this about a love triangle?

When lunchtime arrived, Marge managed a wave of apology to Janette before escaping outside. On an impulse that must have been in the back of her mind all morning, she walked the few blocks to the main branch of First Bank. Marge's First Bank branch was in Factoria, at the base of Newport Hills, where Frank and Lori also banked, but she suddenly decided she should check on the status of one of her certificates of deposit. Plus, by the time she got out of work, her branch office would be closed. It sounded almost plausible.

The CDs rolled over automatically, as she had directed when she purchased them, and would do so until she instructed otherwise, which she intended to do now so she could invest the money in something with growth potential as well as a dividend. That was Marge's excuse for needing to talk with someone. Sailing into the bank, she tried to put a blank, somewhat confused expression on her face. She figured she could impersonate a brainless bimbo with lots of questions about the process. How hard could that be?

After stopping and gazing around the lobby as if she were lost, Marge maneuvered her way past a couple of desks staffed with counselors young enough to be her offspring in order to talk to a stout fifty-something woman. Maybe it was the woman's age that made Marge think she might have more inside information than the younger people surrounding her. Startled at finding Marge in front of her desk, the woman nevertheless invited her to sit. Customer first, Marge thought with an inward smile.

"I heard on the news that one of your co-workers was killed in the park the other night," Marge said after being shown the balance and maturity date of her CD.

The woman's shoulders stiffened. "Yes?" she asked in a tone indicating both the inappropriateness of the question and the finality of the conversation about it. She put her hands on the edge of the desk, getting ready to stand and dismiss Marge.

Tactical error, Marge thought. The counselors young enough to be her children might not have been quite so much on guard.

"How do I change this so it doesn't roll over?" Marge asked quickly. When the woman sat down and opened a drawer to find the proper form, Marge ploughed on. "He must have worked here, at the main branch, didn't he?" She widened her eyes in an effort to look innocent. "I'm sure I understood it was someone in the trust department. That would be here, in the main branch."

The woman sat back and studied Marge with narrowed eyes. When she spoke, her voice was slow and cautious, as if she were running a mental check on each word before uttering it. "Yes, the trust department is here. No, Luke Roddeman did not work here or even for the bank. He was a bank examiner. We have no knowledge about who would have killed him or why they would have done it." She slapped the form and a pen down in front of Marge. "Check where you want the CD amount to be deposited and sign there."

Not a bank employee. Marge thought fast as she perused the form. "Oh, I want to invest this money. Do you have any suggestions? That bank examiner must have made some friends at the bank. I heard he was involved in a love triangle and the other man killed him. Did his girlfriend work here?"

Eyes almost slits, the woman opened a drawer and took out some more papers, handed them to Marge, and stood. "I have no knowledge of this man's personal life. Here is some information about our investment services. I suggest you talk to one of our investment managers. Is there anything else I can help you with?"

"Oh, no thank you," Marge checked to deposit the funds in her savings account, signed the form quickly, and passed it back to the woman. "I'll look over this information and get in touch with an investment manager. Thank you for your time."

Marge left with as much speed as decorum allowed, waving the papers she clutched in her hand in order to cool her face. She wasn't sorry she had stopped the reinvestment of her CD, but she didn't plan on using the bank's investment services. She was ready to take her first plunge into the stock market on her own, using what she had learned in the investment club.

She hoped her skill at investing money proved to be better than her skills as a private investigator. All she had done was demonstrate her ignorance by not knowing Roddeman was a bank examiner and didn't work for the bank itself. The police surely already knew that. Had it been on the news and she was so concentrated on what the reporters were saying about her she had missed it? Or, had she missed the later reports—the ones that mentioned the love triangle?

Why would a bank examiner contact Frank about his mother's account? Was there something wrong with the account? If so, would the examiner call or would he inform the bank officials and they would take it from there? There was a lot she didn't know. Maybe Kate or Robert had a friend in banking who could educate her.

Marge returned to work a few minutes late, although in time to hear Doug announce that there was no more overtime and Wednesday would be the coders' last day. Reviewers' work would finish Friday.

Marge's hands were slow on her reviews that afternoon, but her mind was racing. Why was Luke Roddeman interested in Mrs. Knowles' bank account? What was he going to tell Frank last Friday? How did Frank end up in a motel room in Seattle with Tracy Generas? What was she going to do for money now that this job was ending?

Rather than risk being bombarded with questions from her co-workers, Marge worked through the afternoon break. Plus, she needed the extra time to make up for coming back late from lunch. She couldn't afford to lose even a few minutes since she wouldn't be getting overtime.

Leaving downtown at five o'clock in daylight, instead of after dark at seven, felt like an unexpected vacation. But, it had its drawbacks. The Metro bus was packed at this hour. She stood in the aisle, or rather was held erect by bodies crushing her from both sides, all the way to the Bellevue Park and Ride. After ten minutes of feeling like she was in a straightjacket, a chill crept up the back of her scalp. Marge craned her neck, to the annoyance of those closest to her, and saw several pairs of eyes staring from the back of the bus. She grinned when she recognized Eddie, who gave her a big wink. He often took the same bus that she did. Was it *his* eyes that had given her the willies?

When she was released into the drizzle that had arrived just in time to complicate the evening commute, she collapsed into her Honda and locked all the doors, then waited in line to get out of the lot. She turned on the radio.

"The police have arrested Bellevue computer sales representative Frank Knowles in the bizarre murder of bank examiner Luke Roddeman. Allegedly the murder was the end result of a love triangle involving Roddeman, Knowles, and a woman named Tracy Generas. Police say it appears Roddeman and Knowles met at Kelsey Creek Park to discuss their problem but the discussion escalated into a fight. Knowles allegedly hit Roddeman over the head with the edge of the same shovel he used to dig a shallow grave in which to bury Roddeman. The shovel was found in the park, a few yards from the body. Marge Christensen of Bellevue discovered the body when she saw a hand protruding out of the ground." The report cut away to an interview with a police spokesman, who had no comment. Marge switched off the radio. So much for settling her jitters. She shivered at the possibility she might also have discovered the shovel. But, why take a shovel to the park to discuss a love triangle?

When Marge neared the apartment parking lot, she was surprised to see it was full of cars. Then she saw the reporters with their cameras and microphones at the ready. Fortunately, she found enough room to drive past them and out the other end of the lot before they could determine that she was the Marge Christensen they awaited. Glancing into the rearview mirror, she noticed another car taking the same route she did. Probably another tenant frightened by the sight of all the reporters, or maybe a reporter who had recognized her.

After parking on the street a block away from the back entrance to the apartment building, she waited in the car a few minutes, watching. None of the cars passing in the street slowed. She got out, locked the car, and turned to walk to her apartment building.

Half a block down, Marge spotted the car that had followed her out of the parking lot and saw the shadowy figure of a man behind the wheel. The driver had evidently passed her, turned around, and parked on the other side of the street. As she continued to look at the car, its headlights came on, blinding her and effectively obliterating her view of the driver. She hesitated. Why would someone follow her if he wasn't a reporter? And why would a reporter stay in the car?

There was only one way to find out. She hadn't taken those self-defense classes to be turned to jelly by a car parked across the street. Reaching into her purse for her pepper spray, she pulled herself up to her full five feet six inches and strode toward the car.

With a squeal of tires, the car pulled away from the curb and sped off. Marge tried to get a better look at the driver hunched over the wheel but the car moved too fast. She stood, staring after the car. Had someone wanted to frighten her or had she done the frightening when she charged up with her pepper spray? In either case, why turn the lights on and remain at the curb until she approached the car? She closed her eyes a moment, trying to visualize the car. She didn't know enough about makes and models to identify it.

Marge took extra time to be sure the outer door to the apartment building was locked before running up the three flights of stairs to her apartment. Once inside, she leaned against the apartment door to catch her breath and calm her nerves before listening to the spiel of messages on the answering machine. She deleted three from reporters. She was ready to push the delete button for the next one when she heard the sound of heavy breathing followed by a hoarse whisper. "Stay out of it, Marge Christensen. I know where you live. I know where you work."

Marge collapsed onto a dining room chair, trying to convince herself that her shaking was from the stair climb. The answering machine ran through four more messages, from Kate, Robert, David Walters, and Detective Peterson.

David Walters?

Before she returned any of the calls she went into her studio to get a sketchpad and watercolor pencils. She returned to the table, sat down, and sketched the car that had followed her. Only after she had it on paper was she certain it was an older car, medium-blue, and mid- to full-size. Someone who knew cars should be able to tell the make and model from the drawing. But the license plate was a blur. Could it have been covered with something?

As soon as she had finished the sketch, she called Detective Peterson. He wasn't in, so she left a message. Then she returned Kate's call. She felt the need for a friendly voice.

"Mom? What's this I've been reading in the paper? You didn't tell me the body was buried. And the shovel! How horrible." Marge could hear the shudder in her daughter's voice.

"I wasn't supposed to tell anyone any details, and I didn't know about the shovel until I heard it on the news. At least they've arrested a suspect."

"Frank Knowles? I can't believe it, Mom. I can't even believe he would have an affair. He and Lori were like the perfect couple in the neighborhood."

Marge hesitated. Telling the group at work who didn't know the Knowles was one thing, telling Kate was another thing altogether. But it would soon be public knowledge. The reporters wouldn't stop until they knew everything, and once they knew it they would publicize it.

"Unfortunately, Frank appears to have hit a mid-life crisis," she said. "He has had two affairs since last year, but he promised Lori that he never would again and she believed he was sincere."

"Oh, no! I can't believe it," Kate exclaimed. "Do you think he was having an affair with Tracy Generas?"

"I don't know," Marge said. "I can't think of why else he would be in a Seattle motel room with her when he was supposed to be in Salt Lake City on business. And, it is a strange coincidence that her boyfriend, who is a bank examiner, called Frank for an appointment to talk about a dormant account Frank's mother left at the bank. At least that's what Frank says happened. The news reports make it sound like their conversation was actually about her."

And, this message warning me off lends some credence to Frank's story, she thought.

"That's not on the news," Kate said. "Besides, why would a bank examiner call Frank? Wouldn't a bank employee do that?"

Marge brought her thoughts back to the conversation. "That's what I thought. Lori showed me Roddeman's name on Frank's scheduler. I informed the police before they arrested Frank. I don't think they were surprised, but I still don't know if Lori will ever forgive me. Kate, do you know anyone who can get information about Tracy Generas? I'm wondering if she would lie about something like this."

"I'll check with a friend of mine in the Seattle police

department and see if Tracy's been in any kind of trouble." The excitement in Kate's voice crackled across the telephone line. Marge groaned inwardly. There appeared to be too much of herself in her daughter. "If Lori can get Frank's attorney to delegate it to me, maybe I can follow up to see what I can find out about Mrs. Knowles' account."

Marge hesitated. She didn't want Kate involved in this—not after the threatening phone message. The attorney probably wouldn't agree anyway. Still, offering Kate's help might be a good way to get the attorney to act.

"I'll see if Lori will take my call."

Before dialing Lori's number, Marge called Robert and Caroline to explain to them why she hadn't told them about the hand and to fill them in on all she knew.

"Well, at least you're out of it. The police can take care of it from here on," Robert said.

"But I don't think Frank could have killed anyone," Marge objected, wishing she could be more sure.

"If he didn't do it, the police will find that out, Mother," Robert explained, patience reverberating in his voice. "Please, don't get in their way."

"How is Caroline doing?" she asked to change the subject.

"Fine."

Robert's voice didn't sound fine. Had something happened?

"Really?" Marge asked. "Is there anything I can do?"

"No," Robert sighed. "You might as well know. Caroline had a blood test called a maternal serum-screening, which came back indicating a possibility of Down's syndrome; so the doctors suggested an amniocentesis to be sure. Amniocentesis can cause miscarriage, so I didn't think she should have it done; but Caroline is so paranoid about having a child who isn't one hundred percent perfect that she decided to take the chance." He paused before adding in a barely audible voice, "Since she doesn't want the baby anyway, she'd probably be happier if it had caused a miscarriage."

"Oh, Robert," Marge said, pierced by the pain she heard in her son's voice. "Don't worry about the amniocentesis. I know many women who have had one . . . Wait; you said 'if it had caused.' Does that mean . . . ?"

"Yes, she already did it." Marge could barely hear Robert. "She didn't tell me she had scheduled the appointment. We'll get the results in about two weeks. If she waits that long."

"Robert, if she were going to have a miscarriage from the amniocentesis it would probably have already happened. And she is awfully young for the baby to have Down's Syndrome. Try not to borrow trouble. Wait for the results."

The line went dead.

Marge hung up and took a deep breath to clear her thoughts. She could imagine the anxiety Caroline must be feeling. At least, she would be anxious if she were in Caroline's position. Marge closed her eyes against a wave of regret that her relationship with Caroline was still so strained. She knew Caroline would resist any suggestions or offers of support Marge might give. She wished there were more she could do for Robert. For both of them.

She took another deep breath and tried to put Robert and Caroline's problems in God's hands. With an air of determination, she picked up the phone and dialed Lori's number.

"I can't talk to you right now," Lori whispered. "Frank is here."

"Please, don't hang up, Lori. I have something important to ask you."

"What is it?"

"Kate says that if Frank's attorney would delegate authority to her, she could check into Frank's mother's bank account. I don't want her to do it, but I think your attorney should."

Lori's voice returned to a whisper. "If there were anything there, wouldn't Frank's attorney already have investigated it?"

"I think you should make sure it gets done, that's all. If he's already done it, so much the better."

"All right, I'll see what he's done and, if he hasn't done it, I'll see if he plans to or if they will both agree to let Kate do it," Lori said. She hesitated before adding in a rushed voice, "By the way, Frank was not in the office on Friday. He says someone from the office who sounded like his boss called him and told him to return to Seattle. He flew in late Friday afternoon. Frank says the person told him to go straight to that motel to meet someone, and that someone turned out to be Tracy Generas. But, his boss told him no one from the office called Frank." Her voice dropped to a whisper again. "Got to go. Frank's coming."

After hanging up, Marge settled in her chair to think about what Lori had said. Assuming Frank was telling the truth about the phone call to return to Seattle, who made it? She frowned. Someone deliberately sent him to that motel room and Tracy Generas. But, why would he have stayed there overnight? Either he wasn't telling Lori everything or Lori hadn't passed everything on to Marge.

The phone rang. Detective's Peterson's voice came on the line before Marge had a chance to say anything. "Is it convenient for me to come get that painting now?" he asked.

Marge agreed. After hanging up, she chewed on her lip for a moment. The last call she had to return sent a warm glow through her.

David Walters was a widower who bought Gene's BMW for his daughter's college graduation last year. Marge had found him pleasant and comfortable from the moment they met; she had liked him more than seemed proper for a newly widowed woman. That wasn't a problem at the time, because she thought she would never hear from him again. She did, though. He called to thank her for the drawing of him she had impulsively left in the car for his daughter. And he phoned again, the day after his daughter's wedding a few months later, to see how Marge was doing. Now another call. Marge felt like she was entering unknown territory when she punched in his telephone number.

"I hope you don't think it presumptuous of me to call," David said. Even his voice seemed to have a settling effect. "I've thought about getting together with you several times, but I was afraid going to dinner with me might be uncomfortable for you so soon after your husband's death. From what I see in the papers, it looks like you could use a friendly face. Would you like to join me for dinner on Thursday?"

"I appreciate your discretion," Marge said, cringing at the stilted sound of her words. "I would enjoy having dinner with you and catching up with what's happened with your daughter. I won't ask any questions tonight, though—I'll save them for Thursday."

"Around six?" David asked.

"Around seven would be better," Marge said. "If that's not too late. My current temporary job is in Seattle, so it takes a while to get home and changed."

"Seven it is," David said.

"Oh, you do know I moved, right?"

His laugh brought a smile to Marge's lips. "Yes, but not where. I guess it would be helpful to have your address."

The warm glow intensified after she hung up the phone. Marge had to remind herself to take things one step at a time and to not think about what-ifs. She needed to think about something else.

She wandered into the studio and, for the first time, stared at the painting of the crime scene. She was about to turn away, convinced it had nothing to tell her, when she stopped. How had she not noticed that before? She had resisted looking at what she had painted, that's how. So, she'd missed the dirt encrusted fingernails. And the diamond ring on the victim's finger.

The very large diamond ring.

CHAPTER 5

COULD A BANK EXAMINER afford a ring like that? Why would a murderer leave an expensive ring behind? Did he not see it or did the murderer deliberately leave the man's hand sticking out of the ground? Was it a clue? Were the police meant to see the ring? If so, why?

The sound of the doorbell pulled her away.

"Come in, Detective Peterson," Marge said, buzzing the downstairs door open. When she opened her apartment door to let him in she felt dwarfed by his presence. Perhaps it was the air of authority about him that made her feel delicate when he was around.

"If you are going to keep getting involved in my cases, don't you think you should start calling me Pete?" he asked. His gray eyes actually took on the look of a hurt puppy, incongruous in a man of his stature and bearing.

She grinned despite herself. In the beginning, she had stubbornly refused to call him by his first name. Now, using his surname was such a habit she didn't know if she could change.

"I'll try . . . Pete," she said, but it sounded strange to her ears. "Is that your given name or a nickname?"

"Short for Peter. A gift from my dear demented mother," he said as Marge led him to her small table. He sat and Marge joined him with two steaming cups of coffee.

"Before we look at the painting, now that you've had time to recover from the shock, I'd like to hear again what happened, from the time you entered the park Saturday afternoon and until I arrived on the scene. Take your time and don't leave anything out." He pushed back that shock of hair that refused to stay in place and pulled out a notepad and pen.

Marge concentrated her thoughts on Saturday and related her story for what seemed like the hundredth time.

"Why did you call me instead of 911?" he asked.

"You are the murder investigator for Bellevue," she said.

"How did you know it was murder?"

"I have no idea. Except I can't imagine why else a body would be buried in the park."

"Tell me again what you saw when you lifted the branch."

Marge paused. "I saw a hand sticking out from a blue denim cuff. There was dirt on the hand, and a ring on the ring finger." She glanced at the detective quickly, then away. He gave no indication of being interested in the ring. "The fingernails were caked with dirt." Marge glanced at him again. "I can't honestly say I noticed that, or the ring either, when I saw the hand on Saturday. In fact, I wasn't really aware of the dirty fingernails or the ring until I looked at my painting of the scene a few minutes ago. I painted what I saw without paying attention. When I looked at my drawing this evening, I noticed those details. There was no dirt under the fingernails—just caked on top, more evenly than one would expect."

Detective Peterson nodded. "Your powers of observation are still good. The medical examiner saw the same thing. You say you didn't notice it before?"

"No. I often forget things, but when I draw something, the details come back. My fingers don't forget."

"What do you make of the caking of the dirt?"

You're the policeman, she thought. "I don't know. The dirt was probably what made the medical examiner think he might have tried to claw his way out. But, if that were the case, dirt would have been under the fingernails as well as on top. The only reason there would be dirt only on top would be to make it look as if he had been buried alive; either as some kind of a sick joke or to call attention to something, like maybe the ring."

He gave her a sharp look, making her swallow hard. She knew what the medical examiner thought because she had put herself where she wasn't supposed to be. She breathed a sigh of relief when, after a tense moment, he went back to his notebook. "You mentioned the ring before. What are you trying to say?" he asked.

"It was a diamond, wasn't it? More than a carat, I'd say."

"Almost two carats, yes."

"Don't you think that's a little pricey for a bank examiner?"

Detective Peterson didn't answer for a moment. "It had occurred to me," he finally said. "But it doesn't appear to have anything to do with the murder."

"*If* you have the right suspect and the right motive,"

Marge said. She held her breath. She didn't want to anger the detective so much that he wouldn't listen to her when she had something to tell him.

Detective Peterson sighed deeply. "Assuming that, yes," he said.

"Also," Marge added, "there wasn't any dirt caked on the ring."

Detective Peterson's steady eyes studied Marge. "You think someone put the ring on the finger after he was buried? And caked dirt on the fingernails but didn't dirty the ring? Why would anyone want to call attention to an expensive ring on Roddeman's finger?"

Why, indeed? "Are you telling me the medical examiner didn't notice any of that?"

He grinned, disconcerting Marge. She had never seen him grin before. "No, of course not. We have a very competent medical examiner. I just want to get your take on things; it's always so interesting."

Marge's cheeks burned. He was so condescending! "Maybe you will find this interesting also," she spat, replaying the threatening message on the answering machine. "Someone evidently thinks I have some idea of what is going on." Before he could respond, she handed him the sketch of the blue car. "And this might be interesting, too. This car followed me through the parking lot and sped away when I tried to find out who was driving it."

The concern on Detective Peterson's face as he listened to the message and looked at the sketch gave Marge a feeling of vindication. "Are you sure the car was following you?"

The feeling vanished. "Well, not entirely. But it passed me and then parked across the street from where I parked. When I looked towards it, the driver blinked the lights so

I couldn't see. And when I approached the car, it sped away."

"This is exactly why I asked you not to involve yourself in this case," Detective Peterson said. "If you have put yourself in jeopardy, it is your own fault. But now we have to do something about your safety. Do you have another tape for that machine?"

"Yes," Marge said.

"Okay, I'll take this one and we'll see if our tech guys can get any clues out of it. Is there anything else you can tell me about the car?"

Marge shook her head. "No, that's all I saw in the dark. Even when it sped away, I couldn't read the license plate. I think it might have been covered somehow."

"Okay. I wish you had recognized the make and model, but I know everything you saw is in this picture, so we should be able to make a determination. Although knowing the make and model of a common car won't help much without more to go on. Now, how about a look at that painting?" The detective stood and waited for Marge to lead him to the studio. Once there, he gazed at the painting. When he turned away from it, his eyes rested on Marge again.

"I appreciate that the Knowles are friends of yours," he said. Did Marge detect a note of softness in his voice? "And I assure you the police are investigating this case for any discrepancies. You don't need to involve yourself in order to protect Frank Knowles. You were lucky not to get hurt when you were chasing after your husband's killer last year. But, if Frank isn't the killer and your theories are right, he sounds like one kinky character. You may not be so lucky if you try to outsmart the police and go after him."

"But I haven't done anything," Marge protested. Detective Peterson didn't seem to hear her. He took the two paintings of the crime scene and left.

She frowned. This killer had done some strange things, like calling her after Frank had been arrested for the crime. Did the killer think she knew more than she did? Had she missed something? And, did he think he could scare her off with a phone call?

Returning to the dining room, Marge saw Detective Peterson's jacket, still draped over the back of a chair. Oh, well. She was sure she would be talking with him again.

Marge made a sandwich and changed into comfortable slacks and a sweater, eating half the sandwich as she did. She plastered her rampant curls with hair spray, in a vain hope that they might stay down. As she walked to the door, she grabbed her investment binder and the other half of the sandwich to eat on the way, and hurried down the stairs to her car. The phone calls and Detective Peterson's visit had made her late for the investment club meeting that was held the third Monday night of every month at the clubroom of Melissa's waterfront condo in Kirkland. Holding it in the clubroom meant that no one had to worry about cleaning house, although they did take turns bringing snacks. Thank goodness tonight wasn't her turn.

When Marge arrived at the meeting, Melissa, Janette, and the two other members, Carol Payne and Judith Lemings, had already pushed two card tables together and were gathered around. Only Lori was missing.

"We weren't sure you'd be able to come," Carol said. "We've been hearing about your adventures on the news. Isn't it a shame about Frank Knowles? How could he do a thing like this to Lori?"

"I'm sure he didn't," Marge said, more brusquely than she intended. She sat at the table, picked up the minutes and the treasurer's report, and opened her binder.

"You never know what a man is planning to do," Judith said. "Look at me."

Janette looked at Marge and rolled her eyes. Judith's husband had left her for a younger woman two years before, and Judith never stopped talking about it. She was in the club to try to figure out how she could manage to educate two children and eventually retire with some kind of security with her small salary as a housewife newly reentering the workforce and child support payments that often didn't arrive.

Her bitterness, Marge often thought, was her worst enemy.

"Murder is a bit extreme, you have to admit," Melissa said. "Anyway, it's in the hands of the police and we have business to conduct tonight."

Because the club invested in a variety of strong, well-managed companies, the treasurer's report indicated they were getting closer to the fifteen percent a year gain that was their goal.

"Still, my share will never be enough to educate a child," Judith groused.

"None of us can afford to put in enough each month to expect great gains," Janette said. "But over time, with dividend reinvestment, you'll be surprised at what it will add up to. In the meantime, we're getting a good education on how to handle whatever money might come our way in the future."

Carol, the most timid of the group, pitched in, "I'd be afraid to lose everything if I invested on my own. The fifty dollars we put in each month is one thing; I don't know how you can ever feel sure enough about a stock to sink significant money into it."

"That's what our education about how to research stocks is for," Melissa said. "Still, some people are never comfortable with stocks. And others aren't in a position to invest in stocks. Judith, for example, probably shouldn't invest more than what she is right now because she doesn't have enough to take the risk. People with tight budgets need to find safe places to put their money, even if they lose the opportunity for growth."

"Then, why am I here?" Judith asked.

"To learn how it works, in case you need it someday," Melissa said. "And to understand the different levels of risk in different investments, so that you don't take on more risk than you can handle. We can never learn too much about how to handle money."

That reminded Marge of her trip to the bank at lunchtime. She had to figure out what to do with the $10,000 plus interest she'd be getting from the CD that matured next month. Was she ready to start her own stock portfolio? Carol's misgivings echoed in her mind. Was this money she could afford to risk? What if she lost it?

Marge listened carefully to the analyses Judith and Janette gave on two interesting stocks. She decided to make time to go to the library and continue her own research on both of them. If another temporary assignment didn't come up soon, she'd have plenty of time to do research—and to decide how much of her portfolio she could really afford to invest in stocks.

On the drive home, Marge's mind swam with thoughts of Frank and Lori, her unemployed state on Monday, what to do long-term with her investment money in order to be able to live in some comfort when she was old, and Robert and Caroline's heart-wrenching situation. She needed time to concentrate on each one of these problems. She felt as if she were being pulled apart trying to deal with them all at the same time.

It appeared Detective Peterson was right about one thing, Marge thought when she pulled into the parking lot and had her choice of spots. Media interest in her had died away as soon as Frank was arrested. Thank goodness reporters no longer camped in front of the apartment building.

She had barely gotten inside her apartment and dropped the investment study materials on the counter before there was a knock on the door. Marge started. Who could it be at this time of night? At her door rather than buzzing in from downstairs? She peeked through the eye-hole to see that it was the young woman who lived next door. Breathing a sigh of relief, Marge opened the door.

"Hi, Marianne. What brings you over so late?"

The words came tumbling out as Marge took the florist's box Marianne held out to her. "These came for you while you were out. I was at the door when the delivery arrived. I thought you'd want to get them right away. To put them in water. And to see who sent them."

Marianne almost bounced, unable to contain her excitement. As a single girl, she knew the importance of a box from the florist's shop.

"Thank you so much for accepting them for me," Marge said. "Why don't you come in and have a glass of wine while I find a vase for . . . for . . . for these gorgeous roses," she finished, feeling breathless when she removed the box top and discovered a dozen yellow long-stemmed roses nestled inside.

Before getting a vase, Marge picked up the small card

sitting on top of the roses. "I hope these brighten your days as much as meeting you has brightened mine, Kevin," she read aloud.

"Who's Kevin?" asked Marianne. "When did you meet him? When will you see him again?"

Marge barely heard the questions bubbling from Marianne. She stared at the girl, eyes unfocused, before shaking herself to come back to the present. "Kevin is a man I met in church yesterday. I'll probably see him in church again on Wednesday night." She felt a grin tug at the corners of her mouth. "This sounds like a good reason for you to be in church next Sunday. You never know who you'll meet."

"Uh . . . maybe." Marianne rose to leave.

"No wine?" Marge asked, still feeling mischievous.

"No, it's late. I have to get up early for work tomorrow," Marianne said as she hurried out the door.

Marge shook her head. She didn't understand why so many people, especially young adults, seemed to be afraid of church. For her it was the next best thing to family surrounding her with love and support.

Gently taking the roses from the box, Marge smiled as she arranged them in a vase of water. David Walters and Kevin Lewis, she thought. Two different men, causing two different reactions. What kind of reaction was the right one? Was one of them destined to be the next man in her life? Did she want a next man in her life?

CHAPTER 6

TUESDAY MORNING THE wind kicked in, blowing away the rain and clouds. The sun and invigorating chill, combined with the exercise she had accomplished at the apartment complex workout room before going to work, made Marge feel energetic and hopeful, certain that something positive would happen today. At break time she called Lori at work, knowing she'd be able to talk more freely without Frank around.

"Did you talk to Frank and his attorney?" she asked.

"Yes," Lori said. "Frank is getting scared. He thinks his defense is pretty thin, even though his attorney seems sure of himself. The attorney doesn't think it will accomplish anything to go over the bank papers since they have nothing to do with the case the police have built. He says he doesn't want to waste his time but he won't object to Kate doing it. He's faxing the necessary paperwork to Kate this morning."

Marge groaned when she hung up. She had counted on Frank's lawyer doing this. Would it be putting Kate in jeopardy if she went to the bank? If the lawyer was faxing the papers to Kate, how could Marge tell Kate not to go? Anyway, the killer wouldn't know Kate was doing the research. The killer knew about Marge only because her name was all over the news. Although, the reporters had found Kate. But, it was their job to dig and discover information. The killer wasn't a reporter. Still, she and Kate had the same last name, so how hard could it be? And, the killer might be connected with the bank. What had Marge done, getting Kate involved? Was it too late to put on the brakes?

She called Kate and found out she had already received the authorization. "Can I talk you out of this? I've thought about it, and I think it is too dangerous for you to get involved."

"You're involved, aren't you, Mom? How is that different?"

"Because I'm the mom," she found herself saying. Both she and Kate burst into laughter. Marge gave up, knowing Kate was too stubborn to back off. "But Kate, keep it as quiet as you can. I received a threatening phone call last night. I thought someone followed me home from work yesterday, too, but it was probably my overactive imagination."

"Mother, you have to tell the police."

"I did, but it only made Detective Peterson warn me off again. Besides, what can the police do?"

"If someone wants you to stop poking around badly enough to threaten you, your suspicions may be right. If that's true, your questions are a threat to the real killer. The police should see that, too. At the least, it should make them intensify their investigation."

A chill crept up Marge's back. If only she could believe the police would change their focus. "Maybe this is too dangerous for you to get involved in, Kate. Maybe we can somehow make the attorney investigate the bank. Can't he be accused of negligence or something if he doesn't do a thorough job?"

Kate laughed. "Yeah, something like that. But if he thinks it's a waste of time, how much effort do you think he would put in, even if he did do it? I'll be careful, but I think we have to do this." She said she would call the bank manager and see if she could get an appointment for the next day. "No one else needs to know who I am or what I'm doing," she said. "I'm getting home from work early today. Why don't you come over so we can talk about it and make sure I have all the background? That way I'll have a better idea of what to look for."

After break Marge managed to block out everything except work, holding her concentration throughout the rest of the morning.

"Have you found out any more about the murder?" someone asked at lunch. If Marge had hoped interest would die, she was wrong. No one in this small group had ever been close to a murder before. They were eager to know everything that was happening.

"No, the police are still investigating," she said.

"Some guy was waiting for you when you got off the bus, did you know that?" asked Eddie. "When you got into your car, he ran over to his car and bullied his way into the line close behind you."

"Oh, Eddie, that sounds like something from a mystery novel," cooed a pretty blonde girl.

Marge felt a chill creep through her again. "Did you see what the man looked like?"

"No, I didn't get a good look at his face. As you saw, I was wedged in the back near the window, and by the time I got off the bus you were both near your car. He looked like any other commuter, except he must have been on an earlier bus to be waiting for you like that. If it hadn't been for how intently he was watching you as you walked to your car, I probably wouldn't have noticed him."

"Can you describe his car?" Marge asked.

"It was a Chevy Nova, medium-blue, a few years old."

Marge wished she had brought her drawing. If it were the same car, she would have to drop any lingering hope that it was an innocent person she had frightened away.

"How did you happen to be watching Marge so closely?" Janette asked.

"The murder intrigues me; everything about it is so strange. Since Marge is involved in it, I guess my eyes automatically followed her while I was dreaming up possible scenarios for how and why it happened."

Marge wasn't sure she liked the idea of anyone's eyes following her that closely, no matter how well meaning.

Eddie turned back to Marge, frowning. "The guy waited until you got to your car before running to his. It's almost like he knew the car but not what you looked like, or he knew what you looked like but not the car, so he had to hang around to get the connection before running back to his car to follow you."

If, as unlikely as it sounded, the killer had been in the woods when Marge found the body, he would know what she looked like. But he wouldn't know what car she drove since she hadn't driven to the park.

Marge left the office building promptly at five o'clock, into a fresh onslaught of rain. Ducking the raindrops like the confirmed Seattleite she considered herself to be, she started down the hill toward the waterfront. She was half a block from work when the prickly feeling in the back of her neck started up again. She glanced over her shoulder but had no way of knowing which of the many faces behind her was the cause.

She walked a little farther before stopping to look into a shop window and think. The voice on the phone had said he knew where she worked as well as where she lived. If she were being followed, she would lead the killer directly to Kate's apartment. She couldn't do that. She started to look around for a store where she could lose anyone who might be following her. After that she would call Kate and tell her she wasn't coming. But, before she could move, loud voices drew her attention. Turning, she saw a crowd gathered around a man on a bicycle who was standing over another man lying on the sidewalk. All Marge could see of the man on the sidewalk were his legs; his face was blocked by the crowd.

"Why don't you watch where you're going? Did you see him run into me?" he asked the crowd, his voice indignant. As several bystanders voiced agreement, the man on the bicycle turned and Marge gasped. It was Eddie. He looked at Marge and waved at her. She stared for a moment before realizing he was waving her off. She hurried on down the hill, heart beating fast. She turned right at the next block, right again back up the hill, then left, right, and left before making a final left to head down the hill toward Kate's apartment. She could only hope that by the time the man could get away from the crowd he wouldn't be able to tell which way she had gone.

Eddie had deliberately run into that man. Why was he on a bicycle, when he usually rode the bus? He must have recognized the man that followed her yesterday after all. Should she have stopped to see what the man looked like so they could learn his identity? It was too late for that. She would have to see what Eddie remembered when she got to work tomorrow.

Marge was out of breath when she rang Kate's apartment on the building's security phone. But by the time she reached Kate's apartment she had nearly regained her composure. Kate answered the door and opened her arms in greeting, making Marge forget the scene on the sidewalk for a moment.

Robert and Kate shared their father's coloring but Robert was larger, more deliberate, like Marge's father. Kate not only had Gene's small bones and slight build, her movements and expressions also mirrored his. Marge hugged her close, smiling when Kate whirled back into the gray and white kitchen, compact but open to the dining area, to finish laying out the Teriyaki chicken and steamed rice she had picked up on her way home. Kate's green eyes, more startling in her olive complexion than Marge's were with her creamy skin, were her sole gift from Marge. Except, apparently, her thirst for adventure.

Marge walked to the living room windows. The blinds were raised for maximum exposure to the view from the eighth-floor apartment. Marge felt something inside her open up to the expansiveness. At this time of the afternoon, on an overcast day, there wasn't a lot to see. Lights at the container port far to the left sparkled and shimmered in the mist. Down the hill in front of her, towards the waterfront, haloed streetlights illuminated rooftops. A few windows were lit in nearby high-rises. Even fewer tiny lights twinkled through the haze on the other side of a gray expanse that would be black at night but on a clear day would turn into the glorious blue stretch of Elliot Bay. Marge knew she had to come here to paint—often—because every day this view would be different. How she was going to work this into Kate's and her own schedules she had no idea.

"Have you heard from Robert and Caroline?" Kate asked when they sat down.

"Not since yesterday," Marge said. "Why? She can't have results of the amniocentesis so soon."

"No results yet. Robert was set against her having it. He'd like to hide his head in the sand and pretend everything is all right."

"Are you sure he isn't afraid of what she'll do if everything isn't all right?"

"Maybe. Still, I'd have to know. Even if I decided to do nothing about it, I'd want to know if my baby wasn't going to be normal, so I could prepare."

"What do you think you would do if the baby had a chromosomal problem?" Marge asked.

Kate shrugged. "I don't think anyone can know that until they have to face it. I'd hesitate to bring a child into the world if I felt it wouldn't have a good quality life."

The food Kate had provided turned to sawdust in Marge's mouth. It seemed to her it would be a drastic decision to terminate a pregnancy. How could Kate, her own daughter, talk about it so calmly? As little sympathy as Marge had with groups that bombed family planning clinics and terrorized young girls trying to find the right thing to do, it also bothered her that the idea of terminating a pregnancy could be taken so lightly. Plus, who defined a good quality life?

When they had finished eating and cleaned up the

kitchen Marge struggled to bring her mind back to the purpose of her visit. She and Kate huddled at the table with steaming mugs of coffee, yellow notepads, and pencils.

"Okay," Kate said. "Fill me in so I can plan how to probe into this thing."

Marge did. No matter how many times she repeated it, it didn't make any more sense to her.

After she had related the story, Marge thought for a minute, then decided Kate should know everything, even if Marge hadn't yet figured out what it all meant. "I realized yesterday that the ring I saw on Roddeman's hand was a huge diamond solitaire. The detective said it is almost two carats. I can't imagine that Roddeman could have afforded that on his salary."

Kate looked up from her note taking. "What do the police make of it?"

"They have Frank and they are building their case against him. They aren't looking for other possibilities. Even though Detective Peterson noticed the diamond ring, he doesn't seem to put any significance on it."

"They could have found another logical explanation for it," Kate suggested. "You haven't got much more than supposition here. Still, that threatening phone call makes me believe you are right that something is going on that the police haven't accounted for."

Marge hesitated again before deciding that Kate also needed to understand the risks. "Kate, I'm still not sure you should do this. This afternoon, when I left the office, I thought I was being followed again. In fact, a young man from the office who saw what happened last night also thought so and ran the man down with his bicycle, so I could get away. If looking into this puts you in any danger . . ."

Kate didn't say a word. She stood up and walked over to the cordless phone and brought it back to Marge. "You have to tell the police every time something like this happens," she said. "It sounds like you need protection."

Detective Peterson wasn't in. Marge left a message for him to call and she and Kate went back to work.

Kate took a sip of her coffee. "Before we get into what I can do, I should tell you that my friend in the police department found out a little about Tracy Generas. It's not much, but it is interesting under the circumstances. It seems Tracy is a hooker. She worked the Aurora Strip until about a month ago, and then she dropped out of sight. A day or so ago she suddenly reappeared, sporting a black eye."

"A prostitute." Marge's brow furrowed as she tried to assimilate this new information. "Frank with a prostitute? That doesn't make any sense. Any idea where she went?"

"My friend couldn't get any information out of the other girls on the strip. They don't cooperate with the police as a rule, so he isn't sure if they don't know or aren't telling what they do know."

"I'm sure Lori won't be any happier to hear Frank was with a prostitute rather than having another affair." She shook her head. "But this is too weird—it makes me more inclined to believe Frank's story. I would like to know how Luke Roddeman got involved with a prostitute, too."

"I don't think I can work that into my business tomorrow," Kate said, laughing. "But after I've found out what I can about the account I'll see if I can find an eager gossip to get friendly with.

"Officially, all I am authorized to do is to verify that Frank's mother did have an account with the bank, how much she put in it, how much was in it when she died, and how much is in the account now. If anything appears amiss, I can start making threatening noises about going to the police and see if I can spook out any information about what else might be going on."

"Is there any way you can find out who would have access to those accounts? Or what safeguards are in place to ensure no one who is not authorized can get access to them?"

Kate looked at her. "You should study law, Mom. I can certainly demand to be shown what kind of safeguards they have and how many positions have access, but I'd make you move your accounts out of there immediately if they actually named names. Where are we going with whatever we find out?"

Marge sighed. "I don't have any choice but to confront Detective Peterson with whatever information we get. He's going to be furious if I open my mouth again, unless we come up with something substantial to say."

They batted ideas around for a while longer, even though they both knew they were attempting a long shot with only a slight chance of success and that they wouldn't know their next move until after they discovered what they could learn from this one.

"Why don't you stay here tonight?" Kate asked. "Don't take a chance that the killer is lurking around waiting for you."

"No, I'm not prepared to do that. Anyway, whoever it is won't know what to do since I changed my schedule today. And, in case he waits for me at the Park and Ride, I'll get my pepper spray out of my purse before I leave the bus and keep it ready until I get into the car."

"I'll drive you to the Bellevue Park and Ride and follow you home from there," Kate said.

Marge tried to object, but Kate wouldn't take no for an answer. Kate drove around the Park and Ride lot twice before pulling up beside Marge's car. "Mom, be careful," Kate warned. "I've heard killing is easier the second time; the killer has less to lose after killing once."

That sobering thought had occurred to Marge. "You be careful, too," she said. "Don't stop at the apartment, keep right on driving. Make sure no one follows you away from there. If you think someone is following, drive to the nearest police station. I don't know what I'd do if something happened to you because I got you involved in this."

Marge almost wished for the company of the press around the apartment building. Against Marge's instructions, Kate waited until her mother was inside the building before leaving. Marge watched for a few minutes, but no other car appeared or took off from the parking lot after Kate. With a sigh of relief that no one was tailing them tonight—or at least no one had followed Kate away from here—she scurried into her apartment and bolted the door.

Taking deep breaths to release the tension that gripped her, Marge punched the answering machine to hear the messages it indicated had been left. The first was from Detective Peterson.

"I hope this is not about the case I told you to stay out of," he said before hanging up.

Marge realized that, since he didn't know what she was calling about, he felt no urgency to get in touch with her. She'd have to correct that.

The next message began with silence. Then a husky voice whispered, "Where were you going after work today, Marge Christensen? It better not be to make trouble, because you won't lose me next time."

CHAPTER 7

Marge swallowed hard. She wasn't sure how long she was frozen in place by the words. When she could move again, she checked every window and door in the apartment before phoning the police station.

"Pete Peterson."

Marge tried to stop the shaking in her voice. "I got another call. After someone tried to follow me from work before a friend stopped him with a bicycle."

"Whoa, slow down. I'll come over to hear the tape. You can tell me the rest when I get there."

It was only a phone call, Marge told herself as she waited. No one is in the apartment. Calm down, so you can make sense when Detective Peterson arrives. She picked up a book and tried to concentrate on reading.

A flood of relief almost buckled Marge's knees when she heard the detective's voice on the intercom and buzzed him in. Entering the apartment, he took one look at her, put a hand on her shoulder, and directed her to a chair. "What am I going to do with you?" he asked. "You keep getting yourself into trouble."

The unfairness of the accusation steadied her more than his touch. "I don't understand this. It started before I had done anything, and whoever it is seems to know every move I make. Why does he bother? I haven't found out anything that makes me a threat."

"I think we established at the beginning that we're dealing with some kind of wacko," Detective Peterson said. "Which makes him all the more dangerous. Now, tell me about what happened when you left work today."

Marge explained about how Eddie had stopped the man following her, and that Eddie had seen a man and the blue car, which he identified as a Chevy Nova, in the Park and Ride lot the day before. "I can only think it was the same man; otherwise Eddie would have had no reason to run into him."

Detective Peterson was silent for a long time. "This guy has convinced me of two things," he finally said. "First, we need to put some protection on you. Second, we just might have the wrong suspect. But—Frank Knowles is not off the hook. He could be working with or paying someone to do this; it could be a ploy to divert suspicion from him."

He listened to the tape and established that Marge had still another blank to replace it before removing it and walking to the door. Marge felt a chill at the idea of being alone again.

"You'll be okay locked in your apartment," Detective Peterson said, as if reading her thoughts. "I'll have night patrols drive by frequently. Someone will be watching you from the time you leave here until you get to your office building tomorrow, and if he does his job right you won't see him, nor will this person who's been harassing you."

MARGE ARRIVED at work thirty minutes late Wednesday morning after a night of tossing and turning. She tried to focus her energy on her reviews. It was the only way she could keep from thinking about last night's call, worry about Kate and wonder what Kate would learn at the bank, and agonize over what Robert and Caroline were going through.

When break time came, she found Eddie. "Thank you for stopping that man yesterday," she said. "Was it the same man as the night before? Did you get a look at him this time?"

"Yes, I'm sure it was the same one. I'd recognize him if I saw him again, but I don't know if I can describe him. My memory is poor that way."

Marge pulled a small sketchpad out of her purse and sat across the table from Eddie. He stumbled through a description while Marge tried to translate it onto paper. When she showed the resulting picture to Eddie, he stared at it for a few minutes. "That's close, but not quite. I wish I could tell you what is different, like they do with those police artists on TV shows; but like I said, my visual memory isn't too good."

"That's okay," Marge said. With sudden inspiration, she worked at the sketch again, pulling the bit she could from her own memory, changing the shape of the head and the haircut slightly.

Eddie was excited. "It's still not there, but it's a lot closer. You must have seen him, too."

"Barely . . . just from the back and shadowed from the

side in his car, the night he followed me. I really appreciate you stopping him yesterday. I was going to my daughter's place, and I'd hate to have led him there." She looked at Eddie, puzzled. "What were you doing with a bicycle? Usually you ride the bus."

"I noticed that man leaning against the building and thought he looked familiar. When you came out, he started to follow you, and I realized it was the same guy who followed you at the Park and Ride. I grabbed a bike from the bike rack that someone didn't lock," Eddie said. He looked uncomfortable. "I returned it unscathed; so the owner will never know." The excitement in his voice grew. "You know, we should do something about all this. Maybe we can find out something about Tracy Generas."

Marge stared at the young man. "How?" she asked. She immediately felt guilty for considering even for a moment letting Eddie get involved. It was far too risky for an eager young kid who had no connection with the case.

"She's a hooker, the news said. That means she makes her living out in the open, on the street, probably the Aurora Strip. She has to be out there. Her pimp won't let her stay off the streets. Maybe we can find her."

The blonde was gazing at Eddie with adoring eyes. "You are so smart," she said. "Can I pretend to be a prostitute and help you look for her?"

Marge stared at the girl. "Absolutely not. No to all of it," she said, absurdly feeling like the girl's mother. She looked at Eddie. "You aren't the police and this isn't your problem."

The girl looked crestfallen.

"You're so sweet you wouldn't know how to do it, anyway," Eddie said, touching her cheek to remove the sting of the rejection. "But you," he continued, ignoring the rest of Marge's statement as he looked at Janette, "you are an actress and a beauty. And, you came up through the school of hard knocks. I'll bet you could pull it off."

"No," Marge repeated. "It's too dangerous. This is not a game."

Eddie shrugged. "It was just an idea," he said, winking at Janette. Marge looked at them both hard. Janette's face brightened at the suggestion in a way that worried Marge. Probably fantasizing about the excitement of playing the part . . . surely not seriously considering it, Marge hoped.

By five minutes to five, half of the room was empty. Marge put her last batches of documents together at exactly five o'clock and was out the door within two minutes. She hurried to the bus stop, looking around. No one seemed to be lurking or paying special attention to her. She jumped on the first bus that came along for the free downtown ride. She was to meet Kate at the Red Robin. No one who got on the bus with her got off when she did.

Marge arrived at the restaurant first and was directed to a booth in the warm, dark dining area that hummed with the voices of people relaxing after a day of work. She didn't see anyone else walk in alone until Kate arrived, with briefcase in hand and smartly suited in a conservative medium-gray pinstripe. She and Marge each ordered a glass of Chardonnay, along with a plate of chicken quesadillas to share.

As Marge admired her daughter across the table, she said, "I take it that's your power outfit."

Kate laughed. "One of many," she said. "When you're female and as small as I am, you need all the help you can get."

Marge couldn't wait. "What did you find out?"

"First," Kate paused a moment as their wine arrived, "at a glance, Frank's mother's account seems to be untouched. She deposited twenty thousand dollars twelve years ago. Twenty thousand plus the correct amount of accrued interest is in the account today." She paused again. "I went to the bank manager and asked that he quietly get a detailed statement of all activity on that account for the last twelve years. He said he would get it and messenger me a copy."

Marge frowned, deflated. "So there was no problem with the account?"

"I didn't say that. Looks can be deceiving. Maybe the money was returned to the account after the murder. I told the bank manager I needed to check the account because the beneficiary had heard rumors about some problems with dormant accounts. He hinted that the new bank examiners had indicated an interest in several accounts. That gave me an excuse to ask for the account history and probably explains why he was willing to give it to me."

"Accounts Roddeman was supposed to be checking? What are they looking for?" Marge was still puzzled. "Would a bank examiner be able to embezzle money from the accounts?"

"Not likely, especially since they work in pairs and keep an eye on each other. I was able to find out that Roddeman's partner has been reassigned. Maybe the police can find out where he is and what he knows. Anyway, it sounds as if Roddeman, in the course of his examination, discovered the bank had a dormant account for the deceased Mrs. Knowles. We don't know if or why he tracked down her beneficiary, but Frank said he did. I can't imagine how Roddeman could embezzle money himself, or why he would embezzle money from an account and then call the beneficiary's attention to the account. I also don't know why Roddeman would be the one to inform Frank about the account, since he wasn't a bank employee, unless he didn't trust the bank employees. Nor do I know why he'd make an appointment outside of business hours to discuss it with Frank."

Marge hit herself on the forehead. "I didn't even think of that. Why would Roddeman schedule the call for after-business hours? And in a wooded park in Bellevue, of all places."

"Could be he was afraid of being overheard. Let's say something was amiss with the account and Roddeman found out about it. He might try to discover who the real culprit is before he went public with what he knew. Maybe he thought Frank could help him some way. And, since Frank lives in Bellevue, he thought the park was a safe place to meet."

"I like your logic," Marge said. "Except I suspect banks have an established way to deal with this kind of situation. Anyway, if something was wrong with the account, how and why was it fixed? If Roddeman, and now the new bank examiners, found problems with other accounts, nothing is gained by trying to mask problems with Mrs. Knowles' account."

Kate turned her glass slowly, seeming to concentrate on the movement of the wine against the side of the glass. "Also, if Frank didn't kill Luke Roddeman, then who did? Did Roddeman suspect someone of embezzling money from the dormant accounts? If so, what would the embezzler have to gain by killing Roddeman, since the new bank examiners are finding the same thing? Or framing Frank for the murder and drawing attention to Mrs. Knowles' account? Or is it possible someone not involved with the bank killed Roddeman and framed Frank? Then the connection with the accounts becomes a total coincidence."

"Would making it look like the Knowles' account wasn't involved, by replacing any missing money, mask the connection?"

"Only if Roddeman hadn't contacted Frank. Or if the killer didn't know he had called. Maybe the killer realized no one knew about the Knowles' account and replaced any missing funds hoping it would remain unnoticed, since he was setting Frank up for the murder."

A new idea struck Marge as they left the restaurant. "If we find out Mrs. Knowles' account was corrected after Roddeman was killed, we will know Roddeman was innocent of whatever the problem was. It will also give credibility to Frank's claim that Roddeman called him about the account."

"True," Kate said. "The only problem is the account had nothing to do with the alleged motive for the murder. Finding out that it was tampered with won't clear Frank without something to back it up."

They still had to find Tracy Generas and discover the true motive.

Kate had driven her car to work that morning and parked in her office building's parking garage, which was down the street from the Red Robin restaurant. She insisted on driving Marge to the Park and Ride lot again, both for safety and to save time since Marge was going out for the Bible study meeting later. Marge could see no one following them when they entered the garage and she was certain that if someone saw the two of them go in he wouldn't be able to spot them in the car driving out.

"You don't stay home very much, do you?" Kate asked on the way to the lot.

Marge was silent for a moment. "I'm still not used to it, you know. Even though your father was gone a lot, there was someone else living in the house. I always thought I liked being alone, but being alone all the time and knowing it won't change is different. Sometimes I can get lost in drawing or painting and be fine. Other times I feel so unsettled, so very alone, that I can hardly stand it."

"You can always come over and spend time with me," Kate said.

Marge was already shaking her head. "No, you have your own life to live. I have to find my way, make my life complete on my own terms. After all, you are alone, too, and seem to be fine. It will come. It's just taking longer than I thought it would."

A chill crept up Marge's spine when she walked into her apartment and found the answering machine light blinking. Her finger shook as she reached out to activate the machine. The message began with a familiar silence. "You couldn't stay out of it, could you Marge Christensen? Now I'll have to shut you up, and that daughter of yours, too."

Marge stiffened. How did the caller learn about what Kate was doing so fast? Or who Kate was? Did he work at the bank? Did he follow Kate from the bank? Did he see them together at the Red Robin?

If so, which one had he followed home?

CHAPTER 8

IF THE CALLER WAS trying to frighten her, he was doing a good job of it, especially now that he included Kate in the threat. Marge left a message on Kate's cell phone telling her to be extremely careful. She knew Kate would not pick up while driving. Thankfully, since she parked in a gated garage, Marge was reasonably certain Kate could safely get to her apartment and check her messages.

Marge put in another call to the police station, left a message, and stared at the phone, torn. She should probably stay home, at least until Detective Peterson called her back so she could let him know she was going out. He might want to arrange for her to be followed tonight. Since she hadn't told him she was going out, he probably wouldn't have provided protection for her. But if he didn't call she would have missed Bible study for no reason. She pictured Kevin standing at the door of the church waiting for her.

Kevin? Since when was he part of the equation? The decision was about whether to wait at home for the call or go to church.

"Dumb," Marge muttered, picking up the phone again. That's what cell phones were for. She left another message giving the detective her cell phone number, brushed her teeth to rid her breath of any telltale wine odor, took a hairbrush and tried to whack her curly red mop into submission, and headed out to her car.

Arriving a few minutes late, she locked the car and hurried toward the church.

"Hello, there."

Marge started, felt her knees turn rubbery, and turned to look into Kevin Lewis' pale-blue eyes. Her hands automatically went up to pat down her hair, which felt as if it stuck out in all directions like Little Orphan Annie's.

"Hello yourself. Thank you for the beautiful roses. I can't think what made you decide to do that, but they truly are a day brightener. Why aren't you inside?" Marge clamped her mouth shut before she could chatter anymore.

The amused gleam in Kevin's eyes sent a weak feeling through Marge that made her immediately forget what she had asked. "I like your hair the way it is," he said. "I waited outside for you, since the service hasn't started yet."

Marge kept her hands at her sides as they walked into the vestibule. People were talking in small groups.

"Marge, you naughty girl," Millie cried. "You never told us you were the one to find that body. How could you keep such a thing to yourself?"

"It wasn't something I wanted to talk about," Marge said, struggling to keep her voice steady. "Nor do I want to talk about it tonight. Let's get on with the program."

"But we're your friends, your church family. We're here to help you."

Before Marge could reply, Kevin positioned himself between the two women, took Marge's elbow, and ushered her into the education wing of the church. "Help me what? Feed the gossip mill?" Marge asked. Kevin laughed. Guilt washed over Marge at her unkind remark. This truly was her church family. But there was nothing they could do to help her now, so she didn't want to talk about it with them.

After everyone found a seat in the classroom, Pastor Tom started the discussion. The pastor continued the theme of Job that he had begun Sunday: "Why do bad things happen?" The answers the friends in Job came up with were that it was because people sinned, or because they were being tested, or to give people an opportunity to demonstrate their faithfulness to God. Perhaps the bad things had to happen so something of greater good could follow. Or was it arbitrary, unknowable, a part of the natural order of things?

Marge listened to everyone's ideas and mulled over her own questions about Gene and Luke Roddeman. Before she knew it Kevin was touching her arm and asking, "Why don't we stop at Starbuck's for coffee?" She looked around in confusion. People were already heading out the door. "I can drive and bring you back to your car."

Marge hesitated, her heart beating so hard she was sure he could hear it. Detective Peterson hadn't called back yet, and she felt safer with Kevin than alone in her apartment. If the detective did phone, she could leave immediately. It was only a few minutes drive to her apartment. "Coffee sounds good, but I can't stay long. And, I'd better drive. We can meet there."

"Are you crazy?" she asked herself when she was alone in her car. "You don't even know this man."

"That's why you didn't go with him," she answered herself.

Kevin was waiting at the door for her when she got out of the car at Starbuck's. He ordered latte for Marge and café mocha for himself before they sat at a little round table in the corner.

"So, what did you think about the service?"she asked.

Kevin shrugged. "People do bad things. They pay for it."

"But sometimes people who don't do anything wrong seem to pay," Marge mused, thinking of Gene.

"Are you thinking of that guy in the park?" he asked.

"No. Of my husband."

"Maybe he died for that greater good the preacher talked about."

Marge's head was shaking. "I can't think what greater good can come from someone's death, unless they are truly evil people and the world is better off without them."

"Maybe it's someone who is alive that is being tested," Kevin offered.

Marge shook her head again. "I don't think we can know why bad things happen. All we can do is figure out how to deal with them when they do."

"How long ago did you lose your husband?" Kevin asked.

"A little over a year," she said. "Have you been married?" She glanced at his ring finger, thinking maybe she should have asked this question before now. It didn't look like he had worn a wedding ring, at least not recently.

He shook his head. "I'm sort of a maverick. Never found anyone I wanted to tie myself down for. Yet." The look he gave Marge added meaning to the sentence she wasn't sure she wanted him to intend. "You have children?" he asked.

Marge nodded and briefly told him about Kate, Robert, and Caroline.

"So, you're on your own," he said, nodding as if that somehow pleased him. "You work?"

"Temporary work," she said. "What do you do?"

"I'm in sales. What kind of temporary work?"

Marge told him about her job.

"Is your workplace downtown?" he asked.

"Yes. Why do you ask?"

"My office is downtown, but my position doesn't require me to be there all the time. Still, I'm often downtown. I would like to take you to lunch one day."

Marge laughed. "It will have to be soon. The job ends this week."

"How about tomorrow?" Kevin asked.

That was too fast. "I don't think so. Things are pretty busy right now."

Kevin placed his hand over Marge's. "If you ever want to talk about what happened Saturday, I'm a good listener," he said. She ducked her head, tears threatening. "But," he added, "if you never want to talk about it, that's okay, too." He hesitated, as if waiting for her to say something, before giving her hand a gentle squeeze and then standing.

"Guess we both have to get up for work tomorrow," he said. "I'll follow you home."

Marge followed Kevin out to her car, wondering why she hadn't confided in him. She was tempted. How good it would feel to spill it all out to a sympathetic ear and be comforted. The image of his arm around her and her head on his shoulder sent signals to parts of her body that she hadn't thought would ever be stirred again.

She felt protected as his headlights followed her home. When she signaled to turn into her apartment building parking lot, he sped off with a toot of his horn. The night grew suddenly colder.

Marge spent another restless night. That would teach her to drink coffee so late.

THURSDAY MORNING was a blur. A feeling of finality pervaded the nearly empty room. Doug announced that tomorrow he would finish any reviews not completed by the end of the day. Marge's heart fluttered. She hadn't yet called the temporary agency to let them know she would be available for a new assignment on Monday. Probably because she didn't want to be available on Monday.

When morning break came, she hoped that, despite the distractions going on in her head, she had done a decent job on the reviews she handed in. As agreed, she phoned Kate, but Kate hadn't heard from the bank yet about the details of Mrs. Knowles' account activity. On an impulse, Marge dialed Lori's office number. Lori answered, her voice sounding tired.

"Hi, Lori. How are you holding up?" Marge asked.

"As well as can be expected, I guess."

"Do you want some company this evening?" Marge winced. She had forgotten she was busy tonight. It felt like something she had dreamed, tangled up as it was with everything else.

"No, I don't think so. Frank is still irritated that you pointed the police his way. I know you were trying to help, but it'll take time for him to come around."

"As it turns out, it could be Frank's appointment to talk with Roddeman that leads everyone in the right direction, including the police. Kate has more information to get, but it looks like something funny might have been going on in dormant accounts at the bank."

Marge had to spend the rest of the phone call warning Lori not to get too excited too soon. They didn't have any answers yet.

Marge was late getting back to her work station. Because there were so many reviews to be completed, Marge forced her attention on the job, hardly looking up for the rest of the morning. She didn't realize it was lunchtime until the area around her fell silent and voices came from the break room.

She looked up to see Kevin in the doorway, gazing at her. Her heart lurched.

"Hey," she said, walking over to him, conscious of how frazzled she must look after a morning of pulling at her hair while trying to get her reviews right. "What are you doing here?"

"Well, since we both have to eat, I thought we could do it together."

"Thanks for the thought," she said. "But I hope you didn't go out of your way to come here. I plan on a short lunch and getting right back to work."

A cloud passed over Kevin's eyes before he smiled. "I'll see you on Sunday. Or, maybe call you tomorrow."

To Marge's surprise, Kevin leaned forward and planted a quick kiss on her cheek before leaving. She stared after him, her hand covering the spot, wondering how she was supposed to concentrate on work after that.

The feelings she experienced with Kevin were different than the ones she felt when she contemplated her date with David tonight. David made her feel safe and comfortable. Kevin made her feel . . . excited? Nervous? She wasn't sure; he certainly made her feel something. She tried to push thoughts of both men out of her mind while she worked on the pile of documents in front of her.

The afternoon sped by. Despite working through most of her lunch hour, Marge was late leaving the office and had to wait for the next bus to the Park and Ride. She would have little time to change before David was due.

These days it was a pleasure to go rooting around in her closet to find something nice to wear. She had lost over twenty pounds since Gene died and had given away all her fat clothes when she moved into the apartment. Her closet was filled with clothes from her thinner years that her optimistic self had convinced her to keep. The clothes were like new to her again. And it pleased Marge to think David might find her more attractive than when he first met her.

Because makeup didn't help much with the sprinkle of freckles across her cheeks and nose, Marge didn't usually bother with it. She settled for a swipe of mascara to set off her smoky green eyes and a subtle touch of lipstick. Tonight, of course, when she wanted to look her best, her rampant auburn curls would not be subdued.

When David arrived, the warmth of his presence took Marge's mind off everything else. In the few months since she had last seen him, she had almost forgotten his easy smile and how his blue eyes crinkled in laughter.

As she opened the door wider to let him in, his eyes searched her face with concern. "How are you doing? Have you been able to get past your gruesome discovery?" he asked.

"I'm fine, although I'm not really past it," she said. "The police arrested the husband of a friend of mine, who couldn't possibly have killed that man, so I've been trying to help find other possible explanations for what happened."

The creases surrounding David's gray-blue eyes deepened when he smiled. "If memory serves me right, you had something to do with solving your husband's murder. I hope it's the last time you become involved in anything like this. I should think it would be a bit unsettling."

Marge laughed. "I'll do my best to make this the last one."

It only took a few minutes to drive to the small restaurant David had chosen. By the time they arrived, the light rain had let up completely.

"How is your daughter doing?" Marge asked once they were seated at a table in the dimmed, quiet dining room.

Flickering light from the candle on the table highlighted the softness of David's smile. "She chose well. I think it will be a good marriage. What about your daughter?"

"Her firm is working her day and night," Marge said. "This is fine with Kate, but effectively squashes any chance to meet someone, let alone develop a relationship."

They paused while David approved the wine and the waiter poured it in their glasses. Marge looked up when the waiter moved away. She did a double take. Melissa was walking into the restaurant with a young couple. Marge started to raise her hand to catch Melissa's attention; but quickly changed her mind and dropped it. Melissa was probably working.

However, as soon as Melissa and her party had been shown to their table, Melissa walked over. "Fancy meeting you here," she said.

"I didn't want to take you away from your clients," Marge said as David stood.

"That's okay. They were probably hoping for some time alone to discuss the houses I showed them today."

"Melissa, this is David Walters. He is the man who bought Gene's BMW for his daughter's graduation present."

"Lucky daughter!" Melissa said as she put out her hand.

"David, Melissa Horton. She is the agent who sold my house and has become one of my best friends."

"I'm pleased to meet you." David's voice sounded different. Marge looked at him, then back at Melissa. She felt excluded. The two of them stood for a moment longer, frozen in the handshake, their eyes locked. With what appeared to be a sudden awakening, they dropped their hands and both looked at Marge.

"Well, I'd better get back," Melissa said, retreating abruptly.

Marge looked at David. His head turned to follow Melissa all the way to her table. A stab of jealousy made Marge feel like an adolescent. A future she didn't know she had constructed tumbled around her.

"Don't be silly," she told herself. "You're overreacting. All you planned for was one evening out with David. And, one look doesn't mean anything. Relax and enjoy tonight."

Succulent broiled halibut with raspberry dressing accompanied by crunchy green beans and wild rice pilaf helped. Over dinner they discussed David's daughter's wedding, Marge's children, and in general how life went on when a marriage was cut short by premature death.

They talked at length over after-dinner coffee, long after Melissa had left with her clients. Long enough to allow their easy camaraderie to resurface.

"Thank you so much for a lovely evening. I didn't think about anything unpleasant the whole time," Marge said when David walked her to her apartment door.

He smiled. "That was the idea. I'm glad it succeeded." He paused for a moment, as if he wanted to say something more, but instead said goodnight and left.

Marge leaned against the door after closing it, letting the pleasure of the evening wash over her. The smile was still on her lips when she saw the message light blinking on her answering machine. She started to walk away without listening to the message. Fearing it might be one of the children, she turned back and pushed the button.

"Did you have a nice evening, Marge Christensen? I'm watching you. My chance will come."

Where was Detective Peterson when she needed him?

CHAPTER 9

DESPITE AN EXTRA CUP of coffee at breakfast Friday morning Marge was still groggy when she climbed into her Honda. The rain had returned during the night, leaving a sheen of water on the incline toward the Park and Ride. Marge touched the brake lightly when the Honda began to pick up speed. Nothing happened.

A rush of adrenalin sat Marge up straight. She mashed the brake pedal with her foot. Still no response.

"God, help me," she cried.

She remembered something about pumping the brake. She pumped. Nothing.

The car accelerated. A curve. Tires squealed. Sweaty hands gripped the steering wheel. Panic threatened. "Think," she cried aloud, the sound of her voice steadying her. "Think."

She shifted down. The car slowed slightly, but not enough.

She shifted down again. The decrease in speed was too little. She was rapidly approaching the car in front of her. With a shaky hand, she managed to push on her emergency lights.

Emergency brake. She grasped the wheel so hard with her left hand that her knuckles turned white. With her right hand she grabbed the emergency brake and pulled it. The Honda jerked, slowed. The car in front began to pull ahead. A burning smell irritated her nose. The Honda picked up speed. "It didn't hold," she cried. "What else? Think, stupid."

Turn off the ignition.

No, don't turn off the ignition.

She gripped the wheel with both hands. Leaned against a curve. Urged the car to stay on the road. She glanced left and right. Too many trees, too much traffic. No end to the downward slope until the main intersection up ahead.

Would the panic button work, warning other drivers? She reached for it. The Honda swerved into a lane of oncoming traffic. Marge grabbed the wheel with both hands and pulled back into her own lane. The sound of car horns receded into the distance behind her. They triggered another wave of panic.

She saw a shallow clearing ahead, off to the right. If she could get to it before ramming the car in front of her . . . it was now or never.

Almost even with the clearing. Marge shifted into neutral and turned the steering wheel hard to the right. The Honda careened off the road, spinning. She kept the wheel pressed hard to the right, willing the car to keep spinning until it came to a complete stop. The car slid off the clearing and into the trees beside it. Branches slapped against the window. A tree trunk scraped the door. A thud and a jerk flung Marge against her seatbelt before the airbag slammed into her face, snapping her back against the headrest.

Marge opened her eyes to see several faces peering in the window at her. How long had she been out? What was that awful smell?

"Are you all right?"

"Can you move?"

Marge wiggled her toes and her fingers. They seemed to be in working order.

"No, no, don't move until the medics get here," another voice yelled. Marge was happy to be told not to move after all. She closed her eyes and drifted back into the fuzz. What was that awful smell?

"Wake up. Don't sleep. You may have a concussion," someone hollered. Marge frowned. Why couldn't they make up their minds?

Sirens. Barked orders. Hands checked her over, pulled her carefully from the car, and placed her on a gurney.

"I'm okay," she mumbled, attempting to rise. Disembodied hands gently laid her back down again. "The smell . . . the smell."

A gentle tap on her cheek triggered a pain that startled her. "Don't sleep," a voice said.

"I'm not," she tried to say, but her voice wouldn't work and her eyes refused to stay open.

Marge's eyes suddenly opened wide to the grays and whites of the emergency room. "My car," she said. "How is my car?" Her voice sounded strangely nasal. She reached a hand to her nose. It felt swollen.

A nurse appeared, breaking up the sterility of the room with her brightly flowered smock. "I don't know anything about your car, but you are fine. A slight concussion. You'll have a few aches and pains for awhile, but no serious damage. Your nose got a pretty good hit from the airbag, but no bones are broken. You were lucky. Facial injuries from that kind of crash can be severe."

Marge smiled and immediately regretted it. "Ow, that hurts. Does my face look as bad as it feels?"

"Probably," she heard from the door. Detective Peterson entered the room with a policewoman. "Your car is being towed to a garage," he said. "The traffic officer is here to take your statement."

"My statement?" Marge asked.

"Which you will need for insurance," he added.

"Do you have any idea how fast you were going?" the officer asked, pencil poised.

"Before or after my brakes failed?" Marge retorted.

"Exactly how did you land in that ditch?" the police-woman asked.

"My brakes didn't work," Marge repeated.

"So, what did you do?"

"I shifted down. I tried the emergency brake. I put it in neutral and got off the road before I hit the car in front of me. What more could I have done?"

The officer glared at her. Detective Peterson stood slightly to the side, a slight smile on his lips but something altogether different in his eyes. Marge wanted to ask what the policewoman would have done differently but other questions were running around in her head.

"What was that awful smell?"

The policewoman gave her a condescending look. "That's the gas from when the airbag deflated."

"Are you going to check my brakes?" Marge asked.

The policewoman looked at her. Marge shifted her gaze

to Detective Peterson. "Why do you think we need to check your brakes?" he asked.

"I think someone tampered with them," Marge said.

"What makes you think that?"

"They didn't work," Marge said. She took a deep breath and started over when she realized how lame that sounded. "When I had them checked a month ago they were fine."

He nodded. "We're having them checked."

The policewoman broke in. "That was a good piece of driving. A lot of people could have been hurt if you hadn't pulled off that maneuver." She left quickly, as if embarrassed at giving out a compliment.

The doctor arrived, gave Marge a quick check over, and said she could go home but that she had to take it easy the rest of the day.

Detective Peterson escorted her to his car and into her apartment, where he listened to the latest phone messages. "I'm sorry I didn't get back to you sooner. I knew about the last two calls because we are tracing all calls to your phone. No luck so far. It appears the caller is using different public phones. Is there anything you haven't shared with me?"

Marge hesitated. Finally she decided it was too dangerous to hide anything from the detective. "My daughter checked the bank records on Frank Knowles' mother's account. I think the murderer may have a bank connection and Kate's activity precipitated some of the calls."

Detective Peterson glowered at her. "Why is your daughter involved in this?"

"Someone had to check those records, and the police didn't seem to be interested." She couldn't resist taunting him a little. "Frank's attorney thinks your case is so thin he can get Frank off without doing any work. But he gave Kate authority to check Mrs. Knowles' account."

"I'll want to see what she discovered," he said.

"Isn't this something the police should have done? I'm not happy that I've put Kate at risk."

He actually looked uncomfortable, but it only lasted a moment. "What made you think we weren't checking those records? If you would stay out of it, like I asked you to, she wouldn't be at risk." Marge squirmed under his glare. "Nor would you," he said, his voice suddenly husky. "I've increased your surveillance. It will now be constant except when you are at work. I assume you'll be safe there, despite your attempts to put yourself in danger." He turned and strode out the door. Marge had to grin despite everything. He did hate to be proved wrong.

Before Marge could sleep, she called the insurance company and informed them about the accident, arranged for a rental car, phoned Doug to let him know she wouldn't be coming in for work, and called Kate and told her what had happened. "I wanted to let you know I'm okay before you heard it on the news," she said. "And to warn you to be careful. I'll call Robert as soon as I hang up."

"I think you should come and stay with me until this is sorted out," Kate said.

"I'll think about it," Marge said.

She considered Kate's offer after she hung up. If Kate were also at risk, it might be better to stay together. But, if the killer were only after Marge, staying with Kate would put her daughter at unnecessary risk. Besides, Marge found herself stubbornly resistant to the idea of being frightened out of her home.

She called Robert's office only to be informed he wasn't in. When Caroline also proved to be away from her office,

Marge tried their home number. No one answered there, either, so Marge left a message letting them know that, whatever they heard, she was okay. She asked them to call her as soon as they got the message. She hung up the phone, her concern deepening. Where could they both be on a workday? The hospital? Having an abortion? No, they couldn't have the results of the amniocentesis yet.

Sitting in her favorite chair, Marge rocked slowly, trying to quiet her nervous energy. She should have been able to sleep, since she hadn't done much of that last night; instead she could feel the adrenalin flowing through her veins. Nothing held her thoughts for long. They kept circling around the fact that the major part of the case against Frank was based on Tracy Generas' story. They either had to find the real killer and prove his guilt or somehow disprove Tracy Generas' account.

After an unsuccessful attempt to relax by watching TV, she picked up the Seattle phone book and found two listings under Roddeman. She hesitated only a moment before calling the first one.

"Hello. I'm looking for someone who is related to Luke Roddeman."

She heard a gasp on the other end of the line. "Why don't you people leave us alone?" a voice choked. The phone slammed in her ear.

Marge was tempted to call back and apologize, to try to explain herself. She knew from experience how upsetting reporters' calls were. But the voice had sounded too upset. Calling again would only make it worse. Instead, she dialed the other number.

"Who is this?" demanded a deep male voice after she again asked about Luke Roddeman.

"I'm a friend of Frank Knowles." Before the man could

hang up, she hastened to add, "Frank did not kill Mr. Roddeman. I am trying to find something to make the police look harder for the real killer."

Marge held her breath during the silence that followed, hoping it meant the man was considering her words.

"I'm Luke's uncle," he finally said. "What do you want to know?"

"I'm sure Frank Knowles was not involved with Tracy Generas. If he wasn't, maybe Luke Roddeman wasn't, either. What do you know about her?"

"Nothing. She was a complete surprise to us. Luke was engaged to be married and very much in love with his fiancée."

"Do you have any theories about why anyone would want to kill your nephew?"

"None. It must have something to do with his work. Otherwise it doesn't make any sense at all. I don't think I can help you any further."

"Did your nephew seem different in any way the last few days before he was killed? Or did his schedule change in any way?"

"No. If he had problems at work he left them at work. He was methodical, a creature of habit, and as far as I know he hadn't deviated from his normal schedule at all."

"One more question, please. Can you think of any reason why Luke would be in Kelsey Creek Park in the evening?"

"He enjoyed that park. He lives near it, and he went there often to walk and unwind."

"Thank you for your help. Also, I called the other Roddeman in the phone book before I called you. I'm afraid I upset the woman who answered. I want to apologize, but if I call back it will probably upset her more."

"That would be Luke's mother. I'll let her know. And I can tell you, she knows nothing about this woman either."

"Thank you again for talking with me," Marge said. "Be assured I won't bother either of you again."

She limped around the apartment, unable to sit down. It looked like Tracy's story was a complete fabrication from start to finish. Interesting. Hadn't the police talked to the Roddemans? Why did they persist in believing the woman's story? She picked up the phone book again. There was no listing for Tracy Generas. She hadn't expected one. She called Kate.

"Kate, is there any way that police contact of yours can get an address for Tracy Generas?"

"Mom, don't you think you should let this go, before you really get hurt? Surely you've given the police enough reason to doubt Frank's guilt."

"Maybe, but I don't know for sure. If Tracy Generas' story were true, even I would have a hard time believing Frank was innocent of the murder. But Frank claims it's not true, we know it doesn't fit with his usual behavior pattern, and Roddeman's relatives don't believe Roddeman was involved with the girl either."

"Roddeman's relatives? Mom, what have you done?"

"A telephone call. It doesn't matter."

"But, if we can find Tracy Generas' address, the police can find it more easily. Why don't you let Detective Peterson work on this one, now that you've cast doubt on his assumptions?"

"I can't believe Tracy would talk to the police except to repeat her story. We have to find another way to get to her."

Marge didn't think she had persuaded Kate to check before she had to hang up to answer the ring of her intercom, announcing the arrival of the rental car.

Kate called back a few minutes after Marge had settled the details on the car.

"My contact says these girls move around too much to have an address. And he said he wouldn't give it to me, anyway. He agrees that this is not a job for an amateur."

Feeling a little dizzy, Marge returned to the rocking chair and closed her eyes. No one was doing anything substantial to clear Frank's name. Not the police and not his lawyer. She had no idea what more she could do.

The intercom buzzed. Who would be at the door in the middle of the day? Marge answered, thinking it must be Detective Peterson.

"Marge? Are you okay?"

"Kevin! What are you doing here?"

"Taking you for a late lunch, since I'm sure you haven't eaten yet."

Marge realized he was right. She hadn't even thought about eating. Maybe hunger was part of the reason she felt dizzy. "I'm not sure I'm up to going out," she said.

"You have to eat. I can come up and fix you something."

Marge drew a quick breath. "No. No. Give me a minute. I'll be right down."

She changed from her workout sweats to slacks and a lightweight green sweater that brought out the color of her eyes. She made a face at herself in the mirror as she again tried to tame the short mass of curls and wished for the millionth time she could do something about the freckles. But, she supposed neither would be noticed among the colors and swelling that were starting to emerge on her face. Especially that bulbous nose! Putting on wraparound sunglasses to hide the bruising around her eyes, she headed out the door.

Kevin's eyes were full of concern. He gently touched a bruise on her cheek. "I heard the news on the radio. I couldn't go back to work without seeing for myself that you were all right."

"Yes, I'm okay. Sore, evidently a little concussed, but otherwise all right."

"Where to?" Kevin asked when she was seated in his car. "I make a mean pot of soup, if you want to come to my place."

"No," Marge answered quickly, her voice louder than she intended. At Kevin's look of hurt surprise she continued more gently. "No, this will have to be a quick lunch. I'm not sure the doctor would approve of my going out, and I don't know how long I'll last. There's a nice little Thai place nearby. Do you like Thai food?"

"One of my favorites," Kevin said. "Lead on."

Marge gave him the directions and they were soon seated in the cozy restaurant perusing the menus.

Kevin grinned after they had given their orders; Pad Thai for her and Ginger Beef for him. "This is a rather drastic way to get to take you out to eat. Next time just say yes." He paused. "After we parted Wednesday night I realized I never asked if you were involved with someone."

"No. I'm not sure I'm ready to get involved with anyone at this time."

Kevin gave her a smile that sent warning signals tingling up and down her spine. "Good," he said. "I can wait. But tell me, what is going on? Was something wrong with your car?"

Marge hesitated. "It was tampered with," she said. "Somebody evidently thinks I know more than I do about that body I found in the park. I've been getting threatening phone calls, been followed, and now this."

Kevin scowled. "And the police aren't protecting you?" he asked. "What do they think we pay them for?"

"They are doing the best they can," Marge said, feeling unaccountably defensive.

"So, you're going to stop, aren't you?" Kevin asked.

Marge shook her head. So much for comfort. Another person trying to talk her out of what she had to do. "I can't. Frank's wife is a good friend of mine, and she thinks it's my fault Frank has been accused. Since the police seem more determined to prove their case against Frank than to see if someone else could be guilty, I have to do what I can."

"What makes you so sure this friend of yours didn't do it?"

"I'm not completely positive. The only thing I'm sure of is that I don't want to see him railroaded if he didn't. But that's enough about the murder. I know next to nothing about you. What kind of sales work do you do that you can take off in the middle of the day?"

"I work for a brokerage house selling financial planning services. We hold those lunch and dinner seminars you probably get an invitation to every now and then. When we're not holding a seminar our time is flexible."

Marge laughed. "Those invitations arrive with some regularity. I often wonder at the amount of money spent, with the meals and everything. Does it really pay off?"

"Sure does. That's why we keep doing them. Many people don't have any idea how to get started with financial planning, or who to contact. We give them free advice, help them set up a financial plan, and usually end up with some of the business that results from it. We don't force it, and we're quick to refer them to other professionals when we don't provide the service they need."

Marge gave Kevin a searching look. She had never gone to one of those seminars because she was sure they would try to talk her into their product whether she needed it or not. Could Kevin's company be as altruistic as he made it sound? Maybe his group was different, since he definitely was not the type she would expect to be in that kind of position. He looked more off-the-wall than a conservative financial planner. But, he'd probably look different in a business suit than he did in the khaki pants and turtleneck he sported today.

"I also wonder about the people who do financial planning," she said. "If they're so smart, why aren't they rich enough so they don't have to work?"

Kevin laughed. "Did you ever hear that it takes money to make money? Saving enough money to start investing is the hardest part. Especially if you have a mortgage to pay and a family to support."

"And, I suppose knowing how to invest the money when you have it doesn't mean you're especially good at getting it or holding onto it long enough to invest it in the first place," Marge added.

"Too true," Kevin said.

"Well, I don't think I'll be using your services. I'm learning how to save the money and then how to manage it with the help of an investment club."

"Sounds interesting. Can anyone join?"

Marge laughed. "Any middle-aged woman who feels the need to handle her own financial affairs can apply to join my club. There are other clubs out there, though."

Kevin shrugged. "It's probably not for professionals anyway. But I'm glad you found something that works for you."

Their food arrived and they settled into eating. The

atmosphere was suffused with a pleasant tension of excitement and expectation. Marge was certain that if Kevin touched her it would set off sparks.

But, was that right? No, this was definitely going too fast. It had only been a year since Gene died.

Was that a problem? Many people started dating in less than a year. What was she afraid of? Her own feelings?

Probably.

These conflicting thoughts kept Marge tense for the rest of the meal. After dessert and coffee she begged off, truthfully claiming increased aches and pains, and asked Kevin to take her home.

Once alone in her apartment Marge decided to take a long-needed rest. Before sleep came though, she wondered how she could keep her promise to Lori. And how she could locate Tracy Generas.

CHAPTER 10

Marge jumped when the phone intruded on her nap. She picked it up, praying it wasn't another whispered threat.

"How are you?" Lori's familiar voice asked. "I wasn't sure if you'd still be in the hospital. I hope your being home means you weren't seriously hurt in the accident I heard about on the radio."

"That was no accident, Lori. Someone tried to kill me."

"Oh, no. Because of Frank? I should never have let you get involved in this."

Marge ignored the last comment. "Lori, what does Frank say about any relationship with Tracy Generas?"

The floodgates opened. "He says there wasn't any. He says he was told by someone who sounded like his boss to go straight from the airport to meet a woman at that motel. He said it sounded like a big contract might be in the works. When he met the woman he thought she didn't seem quite right for a businesswoman, but she was wearing a suit and carrying a briefcase so he figured maybe she worked her way up and hadn't smoothed out all of the rough edges.

"At some point, the Salt Lake City hotel called Frank with his telephone messages. That's strange, but I suppose if someone set the whole thing up he could have arranged it. Anyway, he called me and talked to Brian. For obvious reasons he was reluctant to admit to me that he was in a motel room with a woman, even though it was on business, so he talked as if he were still in Salt Lake City.

"After that, they had a cup of coffee, and that's the last thing Frank remembers until Saturday afternoon, when he woke up in bed with the woman. He was so confused he didn't try to leave. He took the messages from Salt Lake City the woman gave him and answered them, pretending he was still there because he couldn't figure out what was happening and he was afraid I wouldn't believe him. He claims whatever knocked him out still seemed to be affecting his ability to think, and he's sure he was given something to knock him out again. Otherwise he doesn't understand how it could have suddenly been Sunday and the police were knocking at the door. And, of course he was right, I don't believe him. I mean, he stayed there both Friday and Saturday nights and did nothing with that girl?"

Marge wondered what the police had made of Frank's version of the "affair" with Tracy Generas. Surely it should have cast enough doubt to make them investigate Tracy Generas, especially if they asked Roddeman's family about Tracy, too. It should also be easy enough to check with the hotel in Salt Lake City and verify the forwarded messages. Of course, the police were going in with the preconceived notion that Frank was the killer, so they might suspect he was the one who arranged to have the messages forwarded.

"It seems as if he might be telling the truth. I contacted Luke Roddeman's family. They don't believe Roddeman was involved with Tracy either. This is beginning to look like an elaborate setup. Lori, did you hear on the radio that she is a prostitute? I'm sure she was paid or forced to set up both Roddeman and Frank."

"A prostitute!" Lori exclaimed. "Yes, I heard that, too, but it is too hard to accept. Why did Frank need to be with a prostitute? He had no trouble attracting women."

"No, Lori," Marge said. "Listen carefully. I doubt Frank or Roddeman had anything to do with her. It was all a huge frame."

She paused a moment, something that had been niggling at the back of her mind finally shoved its way forward. "Somehow all this ties in with that dormant bank account. Did Frank know anyone at the bank? Anyone who would know his history and use it to discredit him?"

"Not that I'm aware of," Lori said. "I'll ask him tonight. We have to talk to Tracy Generas."

"I know," Marge said, "but I haven't been able to get a lead on where she is. Kate's police contact won't give us any information. She's back on the streets, that's all I know."

"Then, that's where we have to go," Lori said.

Marge stared at the phone in her hand. This was her sensible friend Lori?

"Marge, did you hear me?"

"You've got to be kidding," Marge said. "What do either one of us know about the streets of Seattle? Especially the Aurora Strip, which is where she works. It's dangerous out there."

"Evidently it's dangerous around here, too," Lori said. "And I recall you doing some not so safe things when you were investigating Gene's death."

Not fair, Marge thought. That was totally different.

"You do what you want," continued Lori. "You're probably not up to it anyway, after the crash; but I'm going out there tonight. I have to find out what happened."

"How are you going to get away from Frank?"

"It's been so tense around our house, he's taken to hanging out at the bar in the evening. I'll leave him a note that I'm at a meeting and be gone before he comes home."

Marge knew the Aurora Strip was the only place they might find Tracy Generas. She also knew there was no way she could let Lori go alone. "How do we get there?" she asked.

Lori answered as if she never doubted Marge would go with her. "Why don't we both drive to the Park and Ride? That way your car won't be by my house to make Frank suspicious. But I don't want to take a bus into the city. Who knows who rides it at that hour?"

Marge restrained herself from commenting on the contradiction. Lori was worried about who rode the bus at night when they were going to the Strip?

"I suppose taxi drivers know where to drop us off? Because I don't know where we can park."

"How will we get back to the Park and Ride?" Marge asked.

"I'll put the taxi company's phone number on my cell," Lori said.

This was truly stupid, Marge thought after she hung up. What would Detective Peterson do if he found out? Which, of course, he would, since she was being watched. On the other hand, the surveillance provided protection for Lori and her. That made it worth risking the detective's displeasure.

Her breath came out in a small explosion. She couldn't back out on Lori. Scrounging around in her dresser and closet, she found an old pair of tights and took in the seams on what was already the snuggest sweater she could find—most of her sweaters were comfortably oversized since she had lost weight. The highest heels she owned completed the outfit—if only she could handle them with her stiff muscles. Camouflaging the scrapes and bruises on her face as well as she could with foundation and compressed powder, Marge slathered on the makeup and surveyed the results. It didn't hide much but it did give her a look that would have raised eyebrows in church. Actually, the bruises probably lent her the most credibility; didn't the men slap the girls around a lot?

A wave of dizziness nearly overcame her. She sat on the edge of the bed until it passed. She could only hope to get through this jaunt without serious ill effects from the concussion.

Once on her feet again, she went to the mirror. She shook her head. The Little Orphan Annie look wasn't working. She settled for tying a vibrant green scarf around her curls, with the ends hanging over one shoulder, and adding a pair of her largest hoop earrings. Staring at her reflection in the mirror, Marge shrugged. It was the best she could do.

Grabbing a swingy shoulder bag, she stuck in her driver's license, some cash, the pepper spray, and a pair of scissors; paused and then tossed in a small sketchpad and drawing pencil. Okay. Now that she looked the part for the Aurora Strip, how did she get from here to there without raising eyebrows at the Bellevue Park and Ride?

Scrutinizing her closet, Marge pulled out a long raincoat with a hood to conceal as much of her disguise as possible until she reached her destination. Raincoats never raised eyebrows in Seattle.

She drove the rental car to the Park and Ride lot, checking her rearview mirror frequently to try to detect if anyone was behind her. Did a police surveillance team still just drive by the apartment, or was someone watching her all the time? She had left a light on in the apartment in an attempt to fool her phone caller. She could only hope it didn't fool the police also. But neither one seemed to be following her. Had the police and her stalker both taken a break?

A taxi arrived at the same time as Lori. Lori had also worn a long loose coat, which flapped open to reveal low-slung shorts and a midriff skimming tank top that exposed a rather large expanse of smooth midsection. Her long brown hair, usually confined to a sedate braid down her back, billowed in a bobbing ponytail.

"Where did you get that outfit?" Marge demanded as soon as they were seated in the taxi. "You look like a teeny-bopper."

"One of Brian's girlfriends left it when she changed at our house," Lori said.

"Where on Aurora do you want to go?" the driver asked.

"Uh," Marge stammered. Would the driver take them where they wanted to go? "Do you know the area they call the Aurora Strip?" She held her breath, waiting.

He stared for a moment through the rearview mirror. "You sure you two want to go there?"

"Yes," she said. "We're working on a case," she added,

hoping she didn't look too much like a middle-aged house-wife who had gone over the edge. Lori certainly didn't.

"Okay, your funeral," said the driver with a shrug. "Sure hope you got backup coming."

Marge didn't answer. Should she have told Detective Peterson? No, of course not, he would have stopped them and Lori would never forgive her. Besides, he had police watching her, didn't he? Anyway, it was too late now.

Standing on the shadowy sidewalk, watching the cab speed away, a damp chill of misgiving swept over Marge while rivulets of perspiration trickled down her back. What did Lori think they could accomplish alone in this part of the city? How would they get a hardened street person like Tracy Generas to talk to them? How would they even know Tracy if they saw her?

Marge clenched her jaw and carefully dabbed the dampness from her face. They had come this far; there was no turning back. Taking off their coats, they looked around. They would need them for the return trip home. Marge spotted a window grating on a gun shop, away from the glow of the streetlights. Rolling the coats together she stuffed them between the grating and the window, hoping they wouldn't be noticed.

It took all Marge's concentration to walk on wobbly knees. Lori swung along, hips swaying, as if she belonged. Marge didn't have a clue what they were looking for. A few clusters of people loitered along the curbs, walking, talking, and laughing. It could have been a normal evening on any street in the city. She appeared to be the most unusual thing there, stopping conversation and drawing stares as they passed. Self-consciously, she tugged at the hem of her tight sweater.

A car pulled up to the curb and a girl in a skintight tank top and short shorts, looking like a high school student who had escaped from home for some excitement with friends, walked over and leaned into the passenger window in a manner that pulled the tank top lower and tighter, exposing anything it was meant to conceal. After exchanging a few words with the driver and popping a few bubblegum bubbles in his face, she slipped into the car before they drove away. Well, that wouldn't happen on just any city street.

Marge looked hard at the girls who remained. They were so young and unkempt, like rebellious teenagers. Tears pricked at the thought of their misguided lives. She blinked them back. No time for that. She accepted the stick of gum Lori offered her, popped it in her mouth, and approached the girls.

"Hey, any ah you guys know Tracy Generas?" she asked, working her jaw and wondering for the first time how the ladies of the night talked. Lori turned away. Marge could see that her good friend, the one who had gotten her into this, was struggling not to burst into laughter.

"Who wants to know?" one asked in a sulky voice.

"I gotta talk to her. Know where I can find her?"

A hard-looking man walked over. "What's going on, girls?" he asked.

They scattered like frightened mice.

"You looking for something in particular?" the man asked Marge, quickly eyeing her up and down in a way that made her tug some more at her sweater. He let his eyes rest on Lori.

"Tracy Generas," Marge managed to squeak out.

"Not mine," he said. "Besides, she only does men. You looking for a threesome?" His eyes never left Lori.

Heat crept up Marge's neck and over her face. Obviously she hadn't succeeded in making herself look like she belonged here, even if Lori had. She struggled to find her voice again. "We only wanna talk to her."

"Why should she talk to you? You a cop or somethin'?" His face registered his doubt at this possibility.

Marge gave up on the street talk and stood straight, trying to stare the man down. "We're not with the police department but we need to talk with her about a police matter." She started to reach into her purse for a twenty, quickly decided against it when the man tensed and moved his hand toward his back. She was sure she couldn't afford whatever the going rate was for information.

"Get lost, ladies," the man said, apparently deciding they weren't worth worrying about. He turned and walked away, shaking his head.

"Marge, that was priceless," Lori said, still choking back her laughter.

"Maybe you ought to try it next time," Marge retorted.

Lori shook her head. "You think faster than I do. And I would probably start giggling and spoil it all."

Marge was too scared to giggle. Where did Lori get her nerve?

They had walked a couple more blocks before spotting another cluster of women. They were older and looked used. Perhaps that's why they wore more revealing clothes and stood in more suggestive poses. They only succeeded in making themselves look trashy. But that was the idea, wasn't it?

Their chatter stopped and all eyes turned on Marge and Lori as they neared. "I'm lookin' for Tracy Generas," Marge said while Lori popped a bubble-gum bubble. "Can you guys help me?"

"That slut," said one of the women, her eyes narrowing into slits. "Anything she can do for you, I can . . . better, too." She frowned. "I didn't think she did women."

"You do know her," Marge cried, ignoring the last comment. She hadn't expected success so quickly. She tried to hide her excitement. "You know where she hangs out?"

"In the shadows, where the johns can't see too good," another said, drawing raucous laughter. "Especially since she got that black eye to go with them grown-out roots."

"So, who did that to *your* face? You got a john?" another asked in a voice that reflected total disbelief.

Marge pushed her sunglasses up her nose and glared at her.

"What you want with that bitch?" the first one asked. This woman wished no good for Tracy. Marge decided to try to make the animosity work for them. "We wanna talk to her about the murder of that guy she was seeing," she said. "We don't think she's telling the truth."

"Damn straight she ain't," the woman said, spitting out the words. "If she could snag someone like that bank guy that got hisself killed, I'm Princess Di come back to life."

"So, can you tell me where she's at?"

"She usually hangs out up by that girlie show." The woman flung a hand toward a theater with signs announcing the erotica within. Several nervous-looking men lurked outside the door. "She can't get no johns unless they're already too excited to wait for something better," she added with an unpleasant snicker. "Sure hope you get her good."

Black eye and hair with grown-out roots, Marge thought. At least they had something to go on. She felt cool threads of perspiration roll down her sides as they walked toward the theater. Marge could hardly believe it when she spotted a woman with a black eye and blonde hair. She couldn't tell about the roots. The woman was dressed in a tight black dress that barely reached her thighs. A deep vee in the front left little to the imagination. Spike heels accentuated shapely legs clad in mesh stockings, with black garter belts visible below the hem of the skirt. She looked like she might have stepped off the screen from one of the movies being shown inside. Clutching the arm of a man who staggered slightly, she approached the door of an apartment building next to the theater.

Marge grabbed Lori's arm and pulled her along, but the couple had been in the building a few minutes before they reached it. The outer door was hanging open, lock broken. Marge peered in, then entered a dimly lit musty hallway and listened. No footsteps. Nothing. They must be in a room already.

Wondering how long these encounters usually took, Marge looked around. No place to sit. She spotted a man sitting in the doorway with his shoulders hunched up, cap pulled low. He didn't seem interested in their presence, but as a precaution she pulled the pepper spray out of her purse along with the sketchpad and pencil. She handed the pepper spray to Lori before squatting in a dark corner, trying to ignore the grime and probable presence of small creatures. Her heart was beating so hard she was sure the man could hear it. Lori squatted beside her.

While she waited, Marge worked on a sketch of Tracy. She barely had time to get a good likeness on paper when the man stumbled down the stairs, peering around as if afraid to see anyone he knew. When his eyes met Marge's they widened in alarm and he skittered away. Marge couldn't help a wry smile at the reminder that she obviously didn't belong there. It was pure luck that they had gotten this far. The man stumbled out the door and disappeared.

A moment later the woman came down the stairs, fluffing her hair. She looks tired, Marge thought. The night was still young. Marge wondered how long she had to stay on the street before her workday was finished.

"Tracy?" Marge said, reaching out a hand to detain the woman. Tracy jumped and tried to get out the door but bumped into Lori, who had moved into the doorway. Lori pushed Tracy back so Marge could get a grip on her arm. "Tracy, we only want to talk to you for a minute. Please."

Tracy stopped and turned around. "Who are you?"

"I'm a friend of Frank Knowles."

Marge was glad she hadn't loosened her grip on Tracy's arm because as soon as she said Frank's name the girl tried even harder to break away. Lori pushed and Marge pulled her back.

"We want to know what really happened. Can we go somewhere to have coffee?"

A wave of panic passed over Tracy's eyes. "No. He'll see me if I leave with you. I can't talk to you. I gotta get back to work or he'll be after me."

"Did he do that to you?" Marge asked, reaching out with her other hand to touch the edge of the bruise around Tracy's eye.

Tracy jerked back. "None of your business," she said. "Let me go before I scream."

"An innocent man is going to go to prison for murder if you don't tell the truth," Lori said. "What did you get out of it that makes it worth killing one man and sending another one to prison?"

Tracy's harsh bark of laughter grated. "Me? I didn't get

nothin'. But dead is what I'm gonna get if I open my mouth. So back off." Marge caught her breath and hung on when Tracy made another lunge for the door. Tracy did have something to hide.

"Can we pay you? How much would it take to get you to tell us what really happened? We could get the police to help you get away from here."

"Hah. The police. They never help people like me."

"Why did you do it? They must have promised you something."

"I do what I'm told. If I don't, you see what happens." With her free hand she indicated the black eye.

"Why did he hit you?" Marge asked.

Tracy relaxed slightly, looked pensive. "I tried to keep something. It was so pretty, I couldn't help it," she said. She jerked again. "I've said too much already. Let me go."

The half open door flew back, throwing Lori against the wall. "Jimmy!" Tracy cried. Marge stared. Even though the likeness wasn't exact, she knew this was the man she had sketched from Eddie's description of the man who had followed her on Monday night. Tracy's pimp? What reason could he possibly have for setting Frank up and killing Roddeman?

"Hey babe, why aren't you back on the street? That john left ten minutes ago." The words were smooth but the voice was dark, threatening. Marge shivered despite herself.

"She was with me. I was about to pay her." Marge reached into her purse.

Jimmy pushed Marge against the wall and grabbed at her purse. Marge managed to twist and pull it back out of his reach, but the scissors she was reaching for fell to the floor. "Tracy don't go with no women," he said, his breath heavy and rotten on her face, the menace stronger as he pressed her hard against the wall. "So, who the hell are you?"

Even as he asked the question, Marge saw his eyes widen with recognition. Her heart thudded harder. He had tried to kill her once, what was to stop him now?

"A friend," Marge managed through her tight throat, maneuvering as much as she was able to for position. She brought her knee up hard. She missed her target as he twisted away but the point of her knee connected hard enough with his inner thigh to make him grunt and loosen his grip before her pointed heel came down hard on his foot. He jerked back and roared with pain.

Tracy had shrunk back against the wall when Jimmy entered. She flung herself toward him, almost colliding with Lori. "No, don't hurt Jimmy," Tracy cried, encircling him with her arms. Lori raised the pepper spray with one hand and grabbed Marge's arm with the other, pulling her toward the door.

Jimmy struggled to free himself from Tracy's protection. By the time he managed it, Marge and Lori were out the door. Lori stopped, turned, and sprayed the interior with the pepper spray. After a wide-eyed glance at each other, they kicked off their shoes and ran. Marge gasped when footsteps sounded behind them. They seemed to be getting closer.

"Ow! No Jimmy," she heard Tracy cry from the doorway. "I didn't tell her nothin', honest I didn't. Please don't hurt me."

If Jimmy was still inside the building, who was following them? Marge tightened her muscles in preparation for a fight as their pursuer's steps drew nearer.

"Marge, stop. It's me, Eddie."

She nearly tripped over her feet when she turned her head to verify that it really was Eddie. Once she spotted his mop top and friendly face she stopped running and pressed her hands against her knees to catch her breath. Lori had slowed, too, and stopped once she realized Marge had.

"Eddie," Marge managed between puffs, "what are you doing here?" The roar of a motor made her lift her head in time to see a medium-blue car speed down the street—the same car that had followed her from the Park and Ride lot. Tracy's pimp must not have gotten much of that pepper spray in his eyes.

"Playing bodyguard," Eddie said, his breathing almost as heavy as Marge's. "But evidently for the wrong woman. Janette is out there getting the lay of the land. I'm supposed to be her pimp. We planned for her to work her way into the group surrounding Tracy and try to gain her confidence. Maybe she would let something slip. Imagine my surprise to see you and your friend here all decked out. In confrontation with the man in the blue Nova, no less. What kind of a plan was that?"

"Are you crazy?" Marge asked. "Why are you two involving yourselves in this?"

He grinned. "Janette and I share a taste for adventure. Here comes a cab. I have to get back and keep an eye on Janette. Now that we know what Tracy looks like, it will be easier for Janette to get close to her, maybe get her to talk."

Eddie hesitated when the empty cab sped past. Another car pulled up and both front doors opened. Marge tensed again, ready for an altercation. The tall form of Detective Pete Peterson emerged from the passenger side. A city police car pulled up behind. The street behind Marge was suddenly quiet.

"What are you up to, Marge Christensen?"

Marge fought the urge to run into Detective Peterson's arms. Then she squirmed like a teenager caught with a forbidden beer. "Detective Peterson," she said, her voice sounding guilty, "how did you know I was here?"

"I've had you under constant watch since you got home from the hospital this morning. Imagine my surprise when my officer reported you were well enough to go out, first for a long lunch with one friend, and then to meet Lori Knowles, both of you dressed to hit the streets. Exactly what did you think you would accomplish?"

"Exactly what we did accomplish," Marge said, defensiveness removing the guilt from her voice. "We found Tracy Generas. Even though we didn't have time to learn much, I think she was forced to set up both Frank Knowles and Luke Roddeman. And, her pimp is the man who's been following me, the one with the blue Nova."

"Set up by whom? And why?" The detective asked. Marge didn't have an answer for him.

"Who is this other helper you've recruited?" he said, directing his gaze on Eddie.

"She didn't recruit me," Eddie said. "And, I've got to get back out there. My other friend doesn't have any protection."

Detective Peterson raised a questioning brow at the driver of his car. That man turned to the officers from the police car. "Take this man in for questioning about his solicitation activity," he said. "And find the hooker that works for him."

Marge stared, her mouth agape, as they grabbed Eddie by the arms and took off down the street. "You can't arrest him," she said. "He's not a pimp and Janette isn't a prostitute."

"We'll be the judge of that," said the plainclothesman. "Anything else you want to share with us?" he asked, turning to Detective Peterson.

"No. That's a good idea, to detain those two. At least it'll get them off the streets. If it's all right with you, I'll take these two back to the suburbs where they belong." At the plainclothesman's okay, Detective Peterson stepped back, looked at Marge, his eyes sparkling wickedly as they traveled up and down. "By the way, where are your shoes?"

Marge and Lori both turned to look back at where they had kicked off their shoes. There was no sign of them. Marge shrugged. "Long gone, I guess." And the coats, too, she decided as he led them to the unmarked car.

The plainclothesman took them back to the precinct office where Detective Peterson had left his car. Pete filled out some forms, evidently taking custody of Marge and Lori. They rode in strained silence until they had crossed the I-90 Bridge and headed into Bellevue on I-405.

"So, what did you learn from talking to Tracy?" Detective Peterson finally asked.

Marge told him.

"Hardly substantive evidence. But that's interesting about the pimp and his car."

"Tracy's words may not be evidence, but it sounds like she did what she did on orders from someone. Probably her pimp, Jimmy. Isn't that enough to discredit her story? Or at least look into it?"

"Would it surprise you terribly to know that the police were already looking into this story of hers?"

"What have you found out?" Lori piped in.

The detective only looked at her.

Detective Peterson dropped Lori and Marge off at the

Park and Ride lot. He saw Lori to her car before following Marge home.

When they reached the apartment he went in with her. At his direction, she played her phone messages.

"That's one for you, Marge Christensen. But don't think a police escort will keep me from getting you the next time. Are they watching that pretty daughter of yours, too?"

Marge drew in her breath sharply. This wasn't the voice from the other phone calls, which she now assumed had been Jimmy trying to disguise his voice. This voice was low, tight, and controlled. Had Jimmy been a go-between, a messenger to keep Marge from recognizing the real killer? Was this the real killer doing his own dirty work?

That possibility was much more frightening.

CHAPTER 11

WHEN DETECTIVE PETERSON dialed the number displayed on the caller ID button, the phone rang and rang with no answer. No surprise.

"I guess you don't need me to tell you your brake lines were cut," he said. "Whoever did it didn't even try to make it look like an accident. He sliced right through them."

"So, doesn't that mean you've arrested the wrong man?"

"Maybe. Or maybe this case brought some kook out of the woodwork who is getting his jollies threatening you. Or maybe Knowles had a partner who's trying to muddy the waters."

"Or maybe the pimp resented Roddeman and Knowles getting free service from his girl and decided to make an example of both of them," Marge retorted. But she didn't believe it. The plot against Frank was much too involved for Jimmy to have masterminded, though he could be the killer. He must be working for someone else.

"The police will figure it out, Mrs. Christensen. You have achieved your goal of making us look closer. Now, please stay out of our way and let us do the rest."

"So that I don't get hurt? I think it is too late for that."

The detective's eyes seemed to soften as he looked at her. "I sincerely hope not," he said as he turned abruptly and left.

In the middle of the night Marge awoke, shaking. She had dreamed again of a hand sticking out of the ground. But when the body was dug up and lifted, the face she saw was Melissa's. Hovering in the background were ghoulish faces laughing at Marge.

Howling wind and heavy rain intensified the anxiety the dream triggered. After a fruitless hour of trying to go back to sleep, Marge got up and pulled a chair close to a window to watch Mother Nature's show. It was a less than gentle reminder that, even though winter may be mild, spring does not come easily to western Washington.

Still unsettled, Marge prepared a cup of coffee and took it into the studio with her. She tacked a fresh sheet of paper onto the easel. After a moment's hesitation, she began to paint.

What emerged three hours later was a picture of Melissa and David, walking in a sunny field, hands joined. They were lost in each other's eyes, as they had been at the restaurant on Thursday night.

She buried her face in her hands, expecting disappointment. It didn't come. Instead, a feeling of release washed over her. Gene had only been gone a year. She had rediscovered herself in that year, an identity still so fragile and tentative Marge would risk losing it again if she attached herself to someone too soon. David was a reminder of what she had lost when Gene died. David was not her future.

After a quick shower to revive herself after the restless night, Marge stared at her reflection in the mirror. The swelling was slowly diminishing on her nose. The bruises on her face were turning a variety of colors, the circles around her eyes darker. Maybe she should try to paint that.

Kate called while Marge was attempting to bring herself fully alert with her second cup of coffee.

"I got it," Kate said, "but it's all gibberish to me. I can't ask for help at the office because this isn't a work project. We need Robert to help us figure out what it means."

"Are you busy today? Should I ask them over if they're free?" Marge found herself eager for this chance to see her son and daughter-in-law, to find out what was happening with Caroline and the pregnancy.

"I have to work until two, but I'd like to have you all come over here later, if that's all right," Kate said. "I know it means you'll have to drive into the city one more time, but I feel safer with you here, anyway. I think you should plan to spend the night."

"I'll think about staying, but probably not. I have too much to do here. And I have to go to Seattle anyway to pick up some things I left at the office and to sign my time card since I missed work yesterday. Doug called to say he would be in today. Shall I bring some food?"

"No, no. Don't bring anything. This is my treat. And drive, don't take the bus. There is plenty of parking around here on Saturday. Let's say early, around four? I'll let you know if Robert and Caroline can't make it."

As soon as she hung up with Kate, Marge picked up the phone again and called Detective Peterson.

"Pete Peterson here."

She breathed a sigh of relief that he was in the office on a Saturday. "Detective Peterson, what can you tell me about my friends Eddie and Janette?" she asked.

"I repeat, if you are going to involve yourself in my investigations, don't you think you should call me Pete?"

Marge grinned, feeling sheepish. "All right . . . Pete," she said. "As long as you call me Marge."

"Marge it is. I understand your friend Eddie was sent home with a warning not to involve himself in police business. I hope he listens better than you do."

"And Janette?"

Pete hesitated. "Tracy Generas appeared in an emergency room last night with broken ribs and deep bruises from a beating."

"Oh, no!" Marge cried. "That was my fault. Didn't you pick up Jimmy for causing my accident?"

"There isn't enough evidence to prove it was him. There are a lot of blue Novas in the city. As far as the beating goes, it's a part of life on the street. If it hadn't been for this, it would have been for something else."

"What does this have to do with Janette?"

"Since she was immediately available, and willing, and the Seattle police decided it was safe, they put her in the hospital room with Tracy. They gave Janette a story about being beaten around the ribs and stomach so no one can see it—which, by the way, is another common street tactic. Maybe Janette can get some of the information you and your friends were looking for."

"Thank you for telling me. By the way, did you talk to Roddeman's family? He was engaged to be married. They never heard of Tracy." She thought about Jimmy and shuddered at the memory of his breath on her face. "Besides, doesn't a pimp usually keep his girls in submission so that quitting is difficult?"

After a long silence, Detective Peterson evidently decided to open up a little. "You read detective fiction, don't you? Actually, yes, he does. We talked to Jimmy about that as soon as his connection came up. He swears all he wants is what's best for his girls. If Tracy was happy with this guy, he wouldn't stand in her way. However, the Seattle police have had two of Jimmy's girls in the hospital, which makes his generosity subject to suspicion, so we checked to see where he was when Roddeman was killed, to be sure he didn't do it as an example to his flock. Unfortunately, Jimmy has a strong alibi for the time of the murder. He was in jail for questioning in the beating of another of his girls."

Marge frowned. There went her theory that Jimmy killed Roddeman on someone else's orders. "But you are still buying Tracy's story," she said. "When I talked to Tracy last night it sounded as if she was ordered to do what she did—and she let it slip that she didn't get anything for doing it. It seems to me you could crack her story if you tried hard enough."

The silence on the other end of the line made Marge nervous. She hurried on before Pete could hang up on her. "You know that my daughter is looking into the records on Mrs. Knowles' account. She's getting an activity history printed out. That is the only account we can access to see if something funny was going on. If something was going on that was worth killing for, it surely involves more than one account. You have the clout to find out about other accounts."

"You've been going on the assumption that Knowles was telling the truth when he said Roddeman called him about the bank account. Knowles could have used Roddeman's connection with the bank to try and lead us right down the path you're following."

Marge began to think out loud. "Kate learned that the new bank examiner was looking at trust accounts to see if there was any suspicious activity. Could you get the results of his findings as a part of your investigation?"

Pete sighed. "Already being done," he admitted. "Now, I have to go."

Marge hung up the receiver. She wished she knew what the police were doing. It might save her some work and anxiety. But they would never willingly share information with her. After fixing a tossed salad with a sourdough roll for lunch, she returned to her easel. Taking the quick sketch she had made of Tracy Generas, she painted a picture of the prostitute. Studying the painting, Marge saw how vulnerable and needy the girl looked. Is that what pushed her onto the street? Under what circumstances could the same thing have happened to Kate? Marge felt an urge to go to the hospital and get Tracy, bring her home, and give her something better to fill the need. She shook her head and laughed at herself. What did she know about rehabilitating girls who had lived as hard a life as Tracy?

Before Marge knew it, it was time to get ready to leave for Kate's. Robert had phoned to say they would stop by to pick her up so she wouldn't have to drive. Naturally, when he walked in the door, the first thing he spotted was Detective Peterson's jacket hanging on a chair back in the kitchen.

"What's that? It doesn't look like one of Dad's," he said, scowling.

Marge was tempted to let Robert think the worst, but

remembered he had troubles of his own so decided it wouldn't be fair to tease him. "It's Detective Peterson's," she said. "He let me use it when I found the body, and he forgot to take it back."

When they walked out to the car Marge was glad to see that Caroline had decided to join them. Marge wasn't sure how things stood with Caroline and Robert.

Robert was morose and Caroline tight lipped on the drive to Seattle. Marge stared at the sparkling expanse of Lake Washington as they crossed over the I-90 Bridge and hopscotched off Mercer Island in the middle of the span. The water didn't have its usual calming effect on her. She couldn't help looking out the back window to see if anyone was following. Like yesterday, if the police were tailing her, they hid themselves well.

Of course, the same could be said for her stalker.

After stopping at the office, they proceeded to Kate's apartment, which was sunny and a little too warm and bright. The sinking sun shone directly in the large windows and sliding glass door that led to the deck, while the glare off Elliot Bay intensified the brightness. Kate had cracked the windows to bring in some cool air and offered to drop the blinds, but they opted to endure the glare in order to enjoy the view.

They settled in the living room with white wine. Marge cringed when Caroline accepted a glass. She wondered if Caroline had a drink because she had already decided to have the abortion—or because she didn't care.

Kate brought out the reports on Mrs. Knowles' trust account. Robert took them to the dining table to pore over while Marge tried to wait patiently.

"Have you thought of any names yet?" Kate asked Caroline. Marge straightened in surprise. How could Kate ask such a question, knowing the situation? On the other hand, what easier way to open the subject? Kate wasn't an attorney for nothing.

Caroline's face showed no emotion when she answered. "I'm probably not having the baby. I don't want to . . ." Her voice trailed off.

Kate's look was studied. "Aren't you a little far along for an abortion?" she asked. Marge wondered when abortion had become such a non-event that people could talk about it calmly.

"That's why I was going to have the baby in the first place. But I can't go through a pregnancy to have a child that will break our hearts and ruin our lives. It's hard enough as it is."

Marge thought she must be imagining the pain that passed over Caroline's face. "Did you consider adoption?" Kate ventured.

"No, I didn't. Why should I go through a pregnancy, with the effect it would have on my body and my life, to bear a damaged child to be a burden on someone else?"

Marge closed her eyes to hide her reaction to the return of coldness in Caroline's voice. She thought of Ralph, the adult son of a neighbor when she lived in Newport Hills. Ralph had Down's syndrome. He always had a smile on his face and never spoke a cross word to anyone. And he painted the most charming pictures. That had caught her attention because while Marge was letting her talent waste away he was illustrating greeting cards and notepaper for family and friends. Ralph was not only a joy to his family, he was a contributing member of it. His parents appeared to feel nothing but pride and love towards him.

"What does Robert think about it?" Marge asked.

Caroline's mouth tightened into a stubborn line.

"Robert!" she spat out the word. "I don't believe for one minute he has considered the ramifications of having a child that's not normal. He wants his son. I have to think ahead for both of us, as usual."

Marge sat up straighter. A wave of grief brought tears to her eyes, surprising her. Son, Caroline had said. The child was suddenly real. *Marge's grandson.*

Yet, much as Marge hated to admit it, Caroline had a point. Caroline might not make the decision Marge would, but when Caroline made a decision it was based on what she understood to be the consequences of her actions. Robert, on the other hand, would make a decision based on his emotions.

Marge contained her tears. This was between Robert and Caroline. She had to bow out of it or she'd find herself in the middle of a divorce that was beginning to look inevitable. Probably be accused of instigating it.

Robert saved her from her own thoughts. "You were right, Kate," he called. "More than twenty thousand dollars was removed from this account three years ago. It was returned, along with the interest that would have accrued in the last three years, three weeks ago."

"Removed three years ago," Marge exclaimed. "I doubt Roddeman had any connection with the bank back then. How long does it take bank examiners to do their job? And, do they return to the same bank repeatedly?" She thought for a few seconds. "Returned three weeks ago. Roddeman was still alive, so the time works for him doing the audit, although I don't know why he would call Frank if he were the embezzler. More likely it was someone who didn't know about the phone call and wanted to hide any bank connection between Roddeman and Frank who did the embezzling." She thought again. "But, if we believe

Frank, along with what we know about Tracy Generas' involvement, it looks like this murder, including setting Frank up for the blame, was planned at least two weeks before it happened. If the murder was to keep Roddeman quiet about the embezzlement, the murderer is also the embezzler and probably works at the bank. Someone who had enough access to not only compute the interest over the three-year period the money was out of the account, but also to get it back into the account."

Marge looked at Kate, feeling a surge of alarm. "And, if it is someone who still works at the bank, that's how they knew you were checking into the account. Don't go back to that bank until this is solved, Kate."

Caroline interrupted. "What do you know about Tracy Generas?"

"She claims she had found a permanent loving relationship with Luke Roddeman. Pete says it doesn't track that Tracy's pimp would let her go, as he said he did, because two of his other girls ended up in the hospital when they tried to leave him."

"So, could the pimp have killed Roddeman to teach Tracy a lesson?"

Marge shook her head. "I thought of that, but Pete says the pimp was in jail for beating one of his girls at the time Roddeman was murdered. It also doesn't make any sense to me that having found someone who would take her off the streets and give her a good life Tracy would risk it by shacking up with Frank.

"Frank says that when he arrived at the motel room, believing he was making a business call, Tracy was wearing a business suit and carrying a briefcase, so it appears to me that Frank was lured there as part of a trap and Tracy was used as the bait."

Hit with a barrage of questions about the motel room, Marge explained what Frank had told Lori. "I thought the killer might have chosen Frank in order to discredit Frank's story about Roddeman's call and the appointment to discuss his mother's account. But it looks like that particular account was restored before Roddeman contacted Frank. So, the killer had already planned to frame Frank. I think we have to assume the killer knew Frank. Lori's going to ask Frank if he knows anyone who works in the trust department of the bank."

Marge frowned. "But, if the account was restored, why did Roddeman want to talk with Frank? By the sounds of it, there were other accounts that hadn't been restored."

Robert scowled at her. "Don't you think you've got the police going in the right direction? Why are you still digging around in this? You could get hurt. And Kate, too."

"Thanks at least partly to Kate finding out about the bank examiner's concerns, Pete contacted the bank to make sure they would follow up with their investigation and inform him of the results. That part of it is being handled by the police now, so Pete did ask me to call you off, Kate."

"Pete?" Kate and Robert asked in unison, as the realization Marge was calling the police detective by his first name finally penetrated.

Marge's face warmed and she scowled in irritation at the telltale redness the warmth would generate. "Detective Peterson," she said crisply. "Don't you think we should be on a first name basis after all this time?"

Kate was laughing, Robert frowning, and Caroline looked bemused. "Be careful, Mother," Robert said. "Don't get involved with that policeman."

Kate laughed even harder and Caroline poked Robert

in the ribs with her elbow. He gave Caroline his what-did-I–do-now look. Marge shook her head, smiling to herself, and decided to ignore them all. She picked up the papers from the table. She would give them to Pete. They surely constituted an incentive to stay on top of the bank examiners.

Kate must have spent most of the afternoon preparing the delicious jasmine rice with skewered zucchini slices, cherry tomatoes, onion chunks, and shrimp, touched with a delicate lemon-based marinade.

"How does a busy attorney find time to do all this?" Caroline asked. "If you bought this pilaf I want to know the brand."

"All homemade," Kate bragged, justifiably proud for someone whose diet a year ago consisted of pizza and other fast food. "It doesn't take as long to cook as it did when Mom was running a family kitchen."

Marge nearly choked on a bite of shrimp. She looked at Caroline but Caroline, with a glance out of the corner of her eye, let it slide. Tears pricked at Marge's eyes and she blinked them away. Robert wanted a family with a stay-at-home wife and mother. Caroline insisted on a life of her own. If Caroline terminated the pregnancy, what was to hold them together? Whatever had brought them together, the end of the marriage would cause hurt and disappointment for them both.

With an effort, Marge brought her attention back to the gathering around the table and kept it there for the rest of the meal.

When Robert dropped Marge off, he came into the apartment and checked to make sure everything was all right. The look he gave Marge before leaving was so sad Marge wanted to take him in her arms and comfort him.

He didn't say anything, though, just turned with a wave and a jerk of his bowed head, as if hiding tears, and closed the door softly behind him.

Marge went straight to bed and, despite everything, fell asleep immediately.

SUNDAY THE CLOUDS returned, weighing like an extra ten pounds on Marge's body which, when she thought about it, still ached from her plunge into the ditch. Her slippers slapped in a jerky rhythm as she stumbled to the kitchen to plug in the percolator. The rhythm was already becoming steadier when she returned to the bedroom to take a long hot shower. Gradually the tight strands of pain in her forehead began to loosen, allowing her to feel human again.

Marge looked with disinterest at her wardrobe, finally selecting warm slacks with a bulky blue sweater. She was ready for spring clothes, but the weather refused to cooperate. Was there any other part of the country where a person wore wool clothes more of the year than in Seattle?

She was relaxing over a second cup of coffee, planning her afternoon art class before heading to church, when the intercom buzzer sounded. It couldn't be Pete again so soon. She didn't even know why the idea flitted through her head before she dismissed it.

"Who is it?" she called into the speaker.

"It's me. Lori."

Lori's voice was so tiny Marge could barely hear her. She unlatched the entry with the buzzer, opened the apartment door, and waited for Lori to reach the top of the stairs. Throwing her arms around Lori, Marge drew her friend into a huge hug before pulling her into the room. Lori didn't return the hug, but seemed to take comfort in it.

"How are you holding up?" Marge asked, noting that Lori didn't look as if she was doing too well.

"I don't know," Lori said with a disheartened shrug. "I had to get out of the house and away from Frank for awhile."

"That's what friends are for," Marge said, leading Lori to the kitchen table and pouring her a cup of coffee. She hesitated a moment, then charged ahead. "How are you feeling about Frank now?"

"It would be a lot easier to believe everything he tells me if he had been honest with me in the past."

"I can understand that. How much have the police told you?"

Lori practically snorted. "Your Detective Peterson is not very forthcoming. You should remember. He never told you anything, even after you badgered him into reopening the investigation of Gene's death."

"Well, I've been bugging him about Frank like I promised I would; and it looks like it might pay off. Before I forget, did you ask Frank to search his memory and his address books for anyone working at the bank who might know him?"

"Yes," Lori said halfheartedly, "but he said he can't think of an employee he's had any contact with outside of regular bank business, and he's not conducted enough business there to know people by name."

"I think Pete could be convinced that the situation in the motel room was a setup, but he needs something to substantiate it," Marge said. "If someone set up both Frank and Roddeman, it has to be someone who knows a little about Frank's weaknesses, maybe someone who would have a reason to choose him to frame, and do it in this particular way."

Lori was shaking her head, but Marge noted that she sat taller and there was more animation in her movement. "I can't imagine who or why anyone would target Frank for something like this."

"It doesn't have to be connected with banking—anyone who would have a serious grudge against Frank. I wonder if your attorney or the police can get a list of personnel at the bank for Frank to look over."

Lori managed a real shrug this time. "I doubt it would do much good, since we don't know anyone who works at the bank, but we'll try anything. So, you really think Frank had nothing to do with that hooker in the motel room?"

Marge wished she could lie and drive Lori farther away from Frank so he couldn't weasel his way back into her good graces. But, for Lori's peace of mind, she was glad she could answer honestly. "I do believe Frank's version of what happened. Everything we've found out about Tracy Generas fits with his account. Besides, being in a cheap motel room with a prostitute doesn't fit Frank. It's not his style."

That brought a smile, albeit a rueful one. "No, suburban housewives are more his style."

Unfortunately, Marge couldn't argue.

Nothing was to be gained by rehashing what they already knew, so she led the conversation into other areas in order to take her friend's mind off the whole thing for a little while. They fell into their standby roles, discussing the safe topics of spring gardening and children and how their stocks in the investment club were faring.

By the time Lori left to go home, the normalcy of the conversation seemed to have had the desired therapeutic affect. The strain was almost gone from her face and her shoulders were nearly squared.

Marge had to hurry to get to the second church service. On the way, she realized Kevin wouldn't know she was attending the later service—last week he had met her at the early service.

Had it only been a week? How could she feel this disappointed at not seeing someone she had only known for a week? Besides, hadn't she decided she wasn't ready for romance? The disappointment shifted to delight when she stepped out of her car and started toward the church entrance. Kevin stood near the parking lot, evidently waiting for her.

"How did you know which service I'd be attending?" she asked when she reached the steps. Surely he hadn't waited around when she didn't show up for the early one.

"ESP," he said, his eyes challenging her to contradict him.

She didn't have time, since the service was about to begin. They entered to the resounding chords of organ music and maintained their side-by-side silence.

"Sufficient unto the day is the evil thereof."

Isn't that the truth, Marge thought. She was soon lost to her surroundings, back into Frank's problems and Lori's dilemma, Robert and Caroline's decision, even her own unemployed state. She certainly couldn't stop wondering what the future held, or try to influence it, but she had to guard against borrowing trouble when she already had plenty on her plate.

"I thought we'd pick up some subs for lunch and have a picnic in the park," Kevin said, standing beside the pew.

Marge blinked and looked at him. She'd been so lost in her thoughts she missed the last hymn and the postlude altogether. "Oh, I can't. I have an art lesson this afternoon."

"But, you promised me a meal today." His hand clutched Marge's arm. He immediately let go and rubbed the spot lightly, as if to erase the pressure of his fingers. The rubbing awakened butterflies in Marge's stomach, causing her more consternation than the grip that preceded it.

"I'm sorry," he said, his face rueful. "But, I am disappointed. Can we make it dinner instead? You won't have to get up early tomorrow since your job finished yesterday."

Kevin was right. And she was at fault because she had forgotten about her art class when she had tentatively agreed to lunch with him today. "What about your job?" Marge asked. "You still have to get up early, don't you?"

Kevin shrugged. "I don't need much sleep. And it doesn't matter if I arrive at work a little late, either. My hours are flexible."

Having dinner didn't feel right—maybe because it was too close to her date with David. Even if her brief infatuation with David was out of her system, she didn't want to find herself comparing the two. She brightened. "I don't think dinner will work, but what about a movie this afternoon? After my class? That way you don't need to worry about being late, either."

The twinkle returned to Kevin's eyes. "A movie it is. You choose one and I'll pick you up at . . . four-ish? Depending on what time the movie is showing we could still have a bite to eat before or afterwards."

Marge smiled. "As long as it's something light and informal. I'll see you at four."

Once Marge got home, a quick salad took care of lunch before the doorbell announced the arrival of her art students.

After the girls left, she poured a glass of iced tea, pulled on a sweater, and stepped out onto the deck to enjoy the view over the park during a momentary break in the clouds. The art lesson had reminded her she was out of work. She had to call the temporary agency tomorrow to see if they had anything in store for her. But she would not worry about it. "Sufficient unto the day." Wasn't that the intent of the sermon this morning?

Marge caught a movement out of the corner of her eye and turned to see what it was. She peered into the trees that lined the property but couldn't locate whatever had drawn her attention. She shivered, suddenly conscious of how exposed she was. Would her police protector think to watch this side of the apartments, too? Or had that been her police protector, scaring the person he was supposed to protect? Annoyed at the disruption of her life, she retreated inside. She wanted to catch this guy as much for what he was doing to her as for what he had done to Frank.

Pulling out the entertainment section of the paper, she discovered *As Good As It Gets* with Jack Nicholson and Helen Hunt was playing in a downtown Bellevue theater.

Kevin arrived promptly at four. Marge had to grin as he opened the car door for her. The police must think she was a social butterfly—two different men taking her out within days of each other. They'd have no way of knowing she hadn't had a date in the year since Gene's death.

Peering out the window as they pulled out of the parking lot she didn't see anything suspicious. Nor, as usual, did she see her police guard. If the killer was one person, he couldn't be constantly on watch, yet he seemed to know what she was doing most of the time.

The movie was inspiring and funny. Marge felt guilty for laughing so much when Frank and Lori were in such trouble and Robert and Caroline were dealing with their own challenges. But, when she and Kevin emerged from the theater, she felt as if layers of tension and anxiety had been wiped away—and Marge knew it was the best thing she could have done.

Marge vetoed the downtown restaurant Kevin suggested for dinner. She insisted on something quick and informal. Kevin frowned in thought, then brightened. "Ivars. Gene Coulon Park on Lake Washington."

"Perfect," Marge said, and it was. The fish was light and flaky, the ambience open and casual, the view of the lake fantastic.

"Anything new on the murder investigation?" Kevin asked.

"Let's not talk about it and ruin a lovely afternoon."

Kevin smiled; a twinkle of mischief sparkled in his eyes. "So, how about those Sonics?"

Marge laughed, admitted basketball was quite foreign to her world, and they spent the rest of the meal admiring the lake and talking of nothing in particular.

When they arrived back at her apartment building, Kevin walked Marge to her door. He stood for a moment, as if waiting to be invited in. Looking into his intense eyes, Marge felt a tingle run through her. Fear? Excitement? She wasn't sure. But she knew she wasn't ready to take the next step to find out.

"Kevin, this was a wonderful afternoon. Thank you for insisting we go out; it was exactly what I needed. I'll see you Wednesday night at Bible study?"

A slight frown flitted across Kevin's brow, quickly followed by a smile. He leaned forward and kissed her on the cheek, leaving a warm blush where his lips touched, then he lightly kissed her lips. "Until Wednesday . . . or sooner," he said as he turned and sauntered away.

Marge closed the door and leaned against it, her eyes closed. How much longer would Kevin be patient? If only her life weren't on such a roller coaster, it might be easier to deal with feeling like a teenager. And, if she needed proof that David wasn't to be the next man in her life, the difference between her reaction to him and her reaction to Kevin should do it.

She smiled and brushed her fingers across her lips, feeling again the light pressure of Kevin's kiss. The whole afternoon had been perfect. It had been too long since she had simply had fun. Her mind felt open, receptive. Something dropped into it.

CHAPTER 12

"WHAT IF FRANK had an affair with a woman whose husband was insanely jealous? And the husband found out about it?" Marge said out loud. She shook her head.

No. He'd have to be crazy to kill an innocent man for the sole purpose of concocting an elaborate plot to frame Frank for murder. Why not simply kill Frank, instead? Although, the man they were dealing with appeared to be crazy, didn't he? Maybe the problem was that they kept looking for a logical explanation.

And, the killer might have a second motive for the murder: to get rid of Luke Roddeman before the embezzlement came to light. If so, they were looking for someone who worked at the bank, who had enough access to the accounts to embezzle the money, and whose wife (presuming only a man could have murdered and buried Roddeman) had a connection to Frank, either having an affair or close enough to cause her husband to believe she was having an affair.

It took all of Marge's self-control not to pick up the phone and call Pete Peterson. She needed to think this through and be sure it made sense from every angle before risking his displeasure.

Sleep was impossible. She went into her studio and, to calm herself, directed her fingers to paint something pleasant. That proved to be a picture of Kevin Lewis sitting across the table from her at Ivar's, the darkening sky over Lake Washington behind him. She closed her eyes and sighed, remembering the way his eyes turned up at the corners when he looked at her, as if the sight of her brought him pleasure. She returned to bed suffused by the warmth of that look and soon dropped into a deep sleep.

SLOW DRIZZLE was the first sound she heard when she awoke Monday morning. Coffee, a hot shower, a call to the temporary agency to inform them of her availability for work, and some light housework filled the time until she thought it was late enough to phone the police station. Even so, she wasn't at all surprised to be forwarded to Pete's voice mail.

"Please call," was all she could think of to say. She had to give him a reason to return the call. She added, somewhat weakly, "I have another idea."

Marge managed to finish cleaning the apartment before Detective Peterson returned her phone call. "You phoned," was all he said.

Marge couldn't think of any way to approach her request except head-on. "Could you ask the bank for a list of all its employees at the time of Roddeman's murder?"

A pause. "Why?"

"If Frank was framed, he was deliberately chosen. Someone calling himself Roddeman phoned Frank and made an appointment to talk to him about his mother's dormant account, then returned the money embezzled from it. Discrediting Frank's story would be easy to do, because a bank examiner would not be the one to call a customer about an account. Also, none of the other accounts had money returned."

"If Frank is telling the truth about the call. What is this about money being returned?"

"Oh, that's right, you don't have that yet," said Marge. "The printout Kate had of the activity on Mrs. Knowles' account shows that most of the money was withdrawn three years ago, and replaced, with interest, three weeks ago. I have the printouts here if you want them."

"Damn right I want them!"

Marge winced. There was no mistaking the anger in his voice. "Well, don't bite my head off. You knew Kate was getting this information."

"I'll be over this morning."

Marge hung up the receiver and wondered what constituted morning to Pete. It was already nearly noon. Unless he rushed out to his car and broke the speed limit, he could hardly make it this morning.

On impulse, Marge pulled a pound of ground beef out of the freezer and put it in the microwave to thaw. She lightly sautéed onions, garlic, ginger, and chili peppers before adding the ground beef. While listening for the detective to arrive, she browned the meat before adding canned kidney beans, tomatoes, and spices. She didn't know what possessed her to make chili today; but at least it kept her busy while she was waiting for Pete.

She brewed a fresh pot of coffee, split open two sourdough rolls and readied them to warm in the toaster oven. She covered them so they wouldn't dry out before sitting down to wait.

A half an hour later, she gave up waiting and ate a salad. It was better for her than chili, anyway.

A half an hour after that, unable to gather her thoughts well enough to accomplish anything else, she picked up a book to read.

A half an hour after she started to read, Detective Peterson rang the buzzer. When he came into the apartment he looked official but unhurried. He glanced around, as if taking note of Marge's new home for the first time. "You've pared down from the house nicely. Most people end up keeping too much when they move into a smaller place."

"I needed money, remember? I sold everything I could possibly do without." She hesitated. "Is this still morning to you or have you already had lunch?"

"Lunch? What's that?"

"It's what's waiting in the kitchen, if you aren't late because you already ate."

"I haven't had time to eat," he said, sounding eager. "Whatever it is smells great."

With a few last-minute preparations, Marge placed a bowl of chili and two warm sourdough rolls in front of the detective and poured two cups of coffee. Another few minutes were all it took for the food to disappear. Marge was glad she hadn't taken the time to make her connoisseur's version of chili. She might as well have opened a can for all he could have tasted his food. "Excellent," he said. "It's enough to tempt me to listen to more of your theories."

Marge laughed. "If I knew it was that easy I'd have been

plying you with food since . . ." The laughter died. A vision of their first meeting over Gene's dead body hovered between them in the air, silencing her.

"Is that my jacket?" Pete asked, pointing to the coat hanging over the back of the chair.

"Yes. I keep meaning to give it back to you, but I've forgotten every time you were here."

"The phone calls you are getting are coming from phones in different locations, some in Bellevue, some in Seattle. Your caller thinks he's pretty clever."

"Sounds like he is," Marge said.

"You have some printouts for me?" Pete asked.

"Oh, yes," she said, getting them for him. "And another theory, too. But first, did you happen to investigate whether any safety deposit boxes at the bank had been tampered with?"

Pete eyed her and the fresh cup of coffee she placed in front of him and sat back in his chair. "Yes, although they haven't all been checked yet. Where owners could be found, boxes that hadn't been accessed in over a year were opened and the contents compared with what the owners said was in them. They matched, which was not a surprise since no one can get into a safety deposit box without the owner's key as well as the bank key."

"So, you wondered about the ring, too?"

Pete shook his head. "Nothing is missing from any of the boxes we've looked at. It's taking time to find the owners of the remaining boxes. Some of the people have moved, evidently forgetting about the boxes or, like Mrs. Knowles and her account, died without mentioning the box to anyone. We're trying to get a court order to open the unclaimed boxes once we've done all we can to find the owners."

"Did anyone ever see Roddeman wearing that ring before?" Marge asked.

Pete sighed. "I guess it's no use asking you to leave it alone. We have found no record of Roddeman owning the ring. But, that doesn't mean he didn't purchase it, or that he didn't steal it. We have no reports from the bank of missing diamond rings, either."

"Maybe no one knows it was stolen," Marge said. "Especially since there are boxes that haven't yet been opened. With the precautions the bank has in place against illegal entry, it might have been months or years before anyone found out about a theft."

"Right," Pete said. "But keep in mind that discovering it was stolen might only strengthen the case against Roddeman, or more likely a bank employee, as an embezzler. It won't do anything to clear Frank Knowles of murder charges."

"And the trust accounts? Is there a great deal of money missing?"

"Yes. A great deal."

"Do you know how long Roddeman was a bank examiner, and whether he had worked at First Bank in the past?"

"He was a bank examiner for seven years, and this was his first assignment at First Bank." Now that Detective Peterson had actually shared police information with her, the look in his eyes made her feel like he expected her to pull the rabbit out of the hat and solve the case.

"Is there any indication Roddeman had unexplained funds?"

Pete pursed his lips. Marge held her breath, fearing he would decide he had told her enough. When he did answer, she could hear the reluctance in his voice at sharing still more official information. "There is a recent unexplained deposit of ten thousand dollars to an account in another bank with another name, but Roddeman's address. The account was opened at the time of the deposit."

"Is that close to the amount of the missing money?"

"No where near."

"You haven't found anything older? As far back as at least three years?"

"No, not yet."

"I don't think you'll find anything," Marge said. "Roddeman obviously wasn't the embezzler, not only because it would be unlikely in his position but because the embezzlement of Mrs. Knowles' account happened three years ago. I think the person who murdered Roddeman is the embezzler. And I think this is one elaborate scheme to frame Frank for the murder. If the murderer is also the embezzler, which it looks like, he killed Roddeman to throw suspicion off himself and as a trap for Frank. I think the motive for framing Frank has nothing to do with the trust account."

Detective Peterson stood as Marge chewed on her lower lip. "And, I'm sure it had nothing to do with Tracy Generas. She was just another part of the trap for Frank."

"I suppose you've figured out the reason for framing Frank?"

"Maybe. I think the murderer could be the husband of one of the women Frank had an affair with. Pete, we have to get that list of bank personnel. If Frank recognizes one of those names, I'll bet it will be the killer."

"It's a pretty far stretch, from jealousy to murder," Pete said.

"Yes, but we have evidence that we're not dealing with a balanced personality. It makes sense that he would react to his wife's infidelity in an unbalanced manner. I'm sure he deliberately left Roddeman's hand out of that grave to make sure we noticed the ring. Who would think of that as a way to hint that Roddeman was an embezzler? Also, he seems to enjoy taunting me. There was no reason for him to try to frighten me as long as you thought Frank was the murderer. All he succeeded in doing was to convince me someone else was involved."

Pete hesitated. "There is something I haven't told you, because it should be only police knowledge, but if it will convince you to stop interfering with the investigation it'll be worth it. Tracy Generas had several pieces of jewelry, and she says Roddeman gave them to her. No matter how much you theorize, and no matter how many times I agree to follow your hunches, all the evidence points to Roddeman as a jilted lover and Knowles as a murderer."

"Jewelry from where? If Roddeman bought the jewelry, you should be able to find a record of the purchases. Even if a bank employee found a way to get into a safety deposit box, surely a bank examiner wouldn't be able to." Marge had been so sure she was making headway in figuring this out. If she couldn't convince Pete to keep acting on her ideas, how was she going to get him to prove Frank was innocent?

It was Detective Peterson's turn to frown. "Do you know how many jewelry stores there are in the greater Seattle area?" he asked.

Marge sighed, then inspiration hit. "It can't hurt to get a list of the personnel, can it? Frank's attorney can probably get it."

That did the trick. "No thanks, we don't need the defense attorney gathering information we are already getting. I'll give him a copy. What he does with it is up to him. This is a criminal investigation and it's high time you left it to the professionals to handle."

Marge was relieved that the police were getting the list of bank personnel, but she had been warned off one too many times. "It's a little late for that, isn't it? Would you know as much as you do now if I hadn't kept asking questions? I'm surprised you haven't broadened your thinking after what happened with my husband. As long as you insist Frank is the killer, I will be trying to get to the truth. You'd better get used to it."

Detective Peterson's gray eyes were dark and pensive when he looked at her. They reminded her of her father's when she hurt herself doing something she wasn't supposed to do and he was torn between punishing and protecting.

"What makes you think we aren't still looking at other possibilities? Don't expect any more help from the police department in your endeavors, especially not when they seem to be putting you in jeopardy." He strode halfway to the door, stopped, turned back to grab his jacket off the chair, and proceeded out of the apartment without another word.

Marge stared at the chair. The room seemed empty. She shook off the feeling and went to the phone to call Lori. "Lori, ask Frank's attorney to be sure and bug Detective Peterson for the list of bank employees at the time of Roddeman's murder. Detective Peterson says he is getting it, but I know he won't show it to me. He is obligated to show it to Frank's attorney and I want to be sure Frank gets a look at it as soon as possible. If you can talk Frank and his attorney into it, I'd like to be there when Frank goes through it to see if anything connects."

"You sound excited about something."

"I'm pretty sure I know the motive for Roddeman's murder. I need Frank's help to verify it."

"I guess I always knew you'd find the answer," Lori said, her voice lighter. "I take it you had a falling out with your detective, though, since you're no longer on a first name basis."

The anger Marge had been holding in exploded. "He is not my detective. He is the most stubborn, obstinate man I have ever met. I keep feeding him leads and he keeps accusing me of interfering. It's a good thing Bellevue doesn't have very many murders or there would be a lot of innocent people in jail."

Lori was laughing.

"I don't know what you find so funny," Marge complained. "Your husband could be one of those innocent people."

"Oh, no, you wouldn't let it happen," Lori said. "And I appreciate that, even if Frank and your detective don't."

"Stop calling him my detective." Marge objected again, but she felt the heat seeping out of her anger. "Make sure Frank's attorney gets that list."

After cleaning the kitchen, Marge went into the studio but couldn't settle down enough to work. Looking at her students' latest artwork, she decided to surprise them next Sunday by framing and matting their paintings. She'd have to buy readymade frames and mat them herself. That would make a dent in her budget, but it would be worth it to show them how proper displays enhanced one's work.

She remembered there was a small framing shop in a strip mall on the way to the Park and Ride lot. She glanced around as she hurried out of the apartment building to her rental car. As usual, she could spot neither police nor stalker.

Walking from the mall parking lot to the store, thinking about what color matting would work best for the artwork she had selected, Marge almost missed the "Help Wanted, Part-Time" sign in the window.

When the young salesman was free, he led Marge through a work area back to a tiny office. A slender reed of a man, at least seventy, with a weathered face and the lightest blue eyes Marge had ever seen, rose from one of the chairs and held out his hand. Wispy white hair starting far back on his forehead wafted around his ears.

"Joshua Hurly," he said.

"Marge Christensen." Marge shook his hand and they both sat down. "I'm interested in your framer position; but I don't know if I can afford to take a job like this." Marge explained that she was an art major in college but had done little of her own work since. She had always done her own framing, though, in addition to teaching on a volunteer basis at her children's school and the museum, and now she had her own small art class.

"Are you comfortable with your ability to help customers choose appropriate matting and framing, and put it together?"

"Yes, I don't have any hesitation about my ability to do that."

Joshua Hurley gave her a long, considering look. "I'm in a position where I need someone immediately to take care of a framing backlog," he said. "Could you walk in and start doing the work this week? If we both like the arrangement, we can talk about some flexible scheduling should you need to augment your income with other work."

"I'm definitely interested, especially since you are so flexible," Marge said. "How much does it pay?"

"The pay isn't much. Six-fifty an hour to start and, if you stay that long, a review after three months to decide if you leave or I raise you to seven dollars."

That was as much as some of her temporary jobs paid, less than others. "I hope I'm not pushing it, but could you tell me what the prospects are for raises in the future?"

"The employee that stayed with me the longest was up to nine dollars an hour. That took about three years. A shop like this doesn't make enough to pay much more than that, which is why I get mostly students and have a hard time filling the times when students aren't available."

"So, I could never expect to make a living wage at it," Marge mused.

"Not if you have to support yourself with this job," Joshua said. He studied Marge. "Of course, many artists subsist on less in order to pursue their real work. And, if your work is good, I'd be happy to display it here."

"Food for thought," Marge said, rising. "May I buy the materials and make my own frames tomorrow after my work hours?"

Joshua laughed and rose to shake her hand to seal the bargain. "Yes, that is one of the perks of working here. Materials at cost, too."

"I'll see you shortly before ten tomorrow," Marge said.

As soon as she got home, Marge called the temporary agency to let them know she wasn't available after all. If she could pick up a few more art students, maybe sell some of her own work at an art fair or at Joshua's shop, she might find a way to make a living in her own field. It deserved a try, even if she had to spend more of her savings before she started to break even.

Marge forced herself to sit down and eat a bowl of chili for dinner before acting on the ideas that had begun to churn in her head. Put an ad in the paper for more art students. Find out about art shows coming up this summer into which she could enter. Work on building up her portfolio so she would have enough to show. Who knows, she might even find a gallery that would display her work.

Whoa, slow down, she warned herself. We shouldn't worry about tomorrow, but we should be careful not to build up our expectations too much.

She sat down at the table and composed an ad for the local *Town Talk* and printed up a few index cards to post on the bulletin board in the grocery store and the library and anywhere else she could think of to drum up more art students. She could hold a second art class on Saturday afternoons to start, then see if there was enough interest for weekday classes during the summer, depending on her hours at the shop. Tomorrow morning she would investigate art shows.

MARGE REACHED for the ringing telephone on her way out the door the next morning. She hesitated. A glance at her watch told her she didn't have time to answer it, so she continued out into the overcast day. It wouldn't do to be late on her first day.

Her step was light. She had made several calls earlier this morning and found she had time to enter the Kent Arts and Crafts Show and the Renton Arts and Crafts Show. She was too late for Bellevue, but would look forward to entering it next year. She would have to pinch pennies to get the entry fees together, but she would do it.

Marge made a quick stop at the grocery store to put one of her cards on the community bulletin board. She'd deliver one to the library after work.

Joshua Hurley greeted her in the front area of the store,

his fine white hair turned by static into a halo around his face. "Do you have any cashier experience?" he asked without preamble.

"No," Marge admitted, realizing for the first time that would be part of the job, too.

"Not a problem," Joshua assured her. "You'll learn it in about fifteen minutes, I'd guess."

He proceeded to teach her and she did, indeed, feel confident that she could handle the cash register after fifteen minutes. This was good, because the first three customers to come in purchased art supplies. Marge was pleased to be able to ring up the transactions without bothering Joshua, who was working on a complex framing job.

The next customer had a print to be framed. It was a simple task to identify appropriate matting and a frame to enhance the qualities of the print, a harder one to accept the choices the customer actually made. Marge cringed inwardly, but wrote down the information as dictated and told the customer to call in two weeks if he hadn't heard from them, a time frame Joshua had suggested since they often had to order materials for custom framing.

Fortunately, most of the customers who came in for framing were more open to Marge's suggestions. She didn't know how long she would last if she often found the end product of her work unappealing.

Once she was comfortable with the front store operations, she put out the bell for customers to summon her and went to the back room to start framing previous orders. When she saw the backlog of work she thought she might have been a little optimistic in the wait time she had been giving customers. It appeared to be enough to fill a week or two without ordering supplies. Between customers, Marge began chipping away at it, pleased with how, after a little practice, she picked up her pace and felt right at home.

The young man she had met the day before, a student named Nolan, took over at the end of her shift. Marge found ready-made frames attractive enough for her students' work, chose complementary matting for each of them, paid Nolan, and went to the back room to complete the framing.

"I can see I did the right thing in hiring you," Joshua said from behind Marge, startling her. "You do good work, and if you keep up the way you started, you'll have the backlog cleared out before you know it. I work six days a week. If you have any extra time you want to put in on framing, feel free to come in."

After her stop at the library, it was four o'clock before she got home. Marge stowed the framed paintings in the studio closet before returning to check the call she had left on her answering machine in the morning.

"Marge, are you out already? This is Lori. Give me a call when you get in."

Marge immediately picked up the phone and dialed Lori's number.

"Where have you been? Did you start another job already? I was beginning to get worried," Lori remonstrated when she picked up the phone.

Marge explained to her about the new job.

"You'll be glad to know Frank's attorney got a list of the bank employees from the police. Evidently they requested it a day or two ago. He says he would like to talk to you about your theories, so he'd be happy to have you join us when Frank goes over the list—and Frank has raised no objections. If the list arrives tomorrow, we will meet at the attorney's office at two-thirty. Can you make it?"

"I can," Marge promised. "My shift ends at two so I should have time to get there. Where is his office?"

"The same building as Charles Froyell's office. Think you can risk running into him?"

Marge grimaced. Charles had been Gene's attorney, whom Marge, feeling abandoned, had come close to having an affair with before Gene's death. Marge's guilt over the near betrayal had soured any chance for a continuing relationship, so Marge hadn't seen Charles since. She had no idea how she would react to his presence.

"I don't think there is much chance I'll run into him. It's a large building," she said.

The phone rang as soon as Marge hung up.

"Hi, friend," Melissa said. "How about you and me breaking out of the daily grind and getting together one night this week? We haven't had a chance to talk in ages."

"I'd love it." Marge thought momentarily about her stalker. She shrugged. There would be two of them plus her invisible police protection.

"Let's make it Friday, say around six o'clock. We'll hit a bar or two if we feel like it, but find a nice place for dinner around seven." Melissa said. "I'll pretend you're a client so I won't schedule any other appointments that night."

"I am a client," Marge said, laughing. "Or, at least I was. And maybe will be again, eventually."

"I'll hold you to that," Melissa said. "See you Friday."

MARGE DIDN'T realize how tense she was until Lori called the next morning to confirm that the meeting with Frank's attorney was on. She managed to get through the day at the framing shop by staying sharply focused on her work. She was shaking with fear that they wouldn't find the answer on the list when she climbed into her car to drive to downtown Bellevue.

Marge parked and then took two elevators to reach the attorney's suite, where she was ushered into his large and heavily furnished office by an impeccably coifed and manicured receptionist. Frank and Lori sat in matching wing chairs. Frank nodded curtly, his brows knit in a scowl. Lori, looking dwarfed, rose to greet her.

"Marge, this is Frederick Galvan, Frank's attorney," Lori said. "Frederick, Marge Christensen is the friend who seems to be finding all the right answers for us."

Frederick Galvan was tall, broad, and firm; ex-football player was written all over him. The office furniture had obviously been chosen in a scale to match his size. A mass of neatly trimmed dark curls sprinkled with gray framed a square, determined, and somewhat self-satisfied face. Marge was sure he made a strong presence in the courtroom. Frederick walked around his massive desk and held out a hand.

"I'm very pleased to meet you at last," he said, his well-modulated voice filling the room. "I've followed your attempts to prove Frank innocent with interest." His light-brown eyes indicated he also followed them with some amusement.

Marge shrugged and chose to respond to the words and not the demeanor. "I am anxious to see if we hit pay dirt with the employee list."

But first Marge had to answer numerous questions about how and when she came to her various conclusions about the case. It was hard to recreate the thought processes that had led her here. More than that, it was embarrassing to be questioned by an obviously successful criminal attorney who hired professional detectives to do this type of work. Marge heard the note of condescension in his voice throughout the questioning, despite the sharp, acquisitive attention he paid to what she was saying.

When Frederick had asked and Marge had answered his last question, he nodded once and seemed to shrug away any more interest in her theories. "When we go to trial, I will be calling you as a character witness for Frank," he said. "I'd like to meet with you previous to your appearance to go over the types of questions you should expect."

And probably some answers to those questions, too, Marge thought. She wasn't sure she would make a good character witness. She didn't have much that was positive to say about Frank's character.

"Of course, you will need to keep your theories to yourself at that time. I will develop the case as I believe proper to get the best results. I'm sure you understand." This last was delivered with a smile as false as it was wide and white. Marge glanced at Frank, catching a smirk at the attorney's condescension. She had to look quickly at Lori to remind herself why she was trying to help.

"The list?" Marge asked.

The attorney seemed taken aback by her abruptness. Perhaps he wasn't accustomed to having his pronouncements ignored. At any event, he picked up a large manila envelope from the top of his desk and handed it to Frank.

Frank opened it. There was an expectant quality to the silence in the room. Marge discovered she was holding her breath and forced herself to breathe deeply and slowly. She didn't take her eyes off of Frank.

She saw the slight widening of his eyes, the quick sideways glance at Lori, the tightening of his grip that turned his knuckles white. His eyes continued on down the page; Marge saw them traverse across each name, so she knew he was reading them. The tension stayed in his hands and his jaw.

When he finished reading and looked up, Frank's face was white and unnaturally still, his eyes large and guarded. "I don't know anyone on this list," he said.

He's lying, Marge thought, amazement turning her to stone. Why in the world would he lie about something that could, at the least, keep him out of prison and might possibly even save his life?

"Are you sure?" was all she could manage in the silence that stretched after his announcement. Should she accuse him of lying? He would deny it. Then what?

"I'm sure," he said, not a muscle moving in the mask he turned toward her.

Frederick Galvan gathered up the papers and returned them to his desk. He turned to Marge. "You appear to have come pretty close to the mark with your amateur investigations," he said. "Probably there is an embezzler, which most likely was not Roddeman himself. Roddeman may have been killed by the embezzler, or he may have been killed by someone working for Tracy Generas' pimp. But no one at the bank had it in for Frank. He was set up for the murder because he was handy. He had a history."

Marge shook her head. "How could anyone know about Frank's history or his schedule well enough to fake a phone call from his office? Someone had to have been studying him—someone who wanted to hurt him for some reason. Why don't you give Frank a copy of that list so he can go over it when he is more at ease?"

"Oh, no," Frank said quickly, looking at Lori. "I don't need to see it again."

Lori frowned, her eyes puzzled. "What harm could it do, Frank? You might think of something."

"No, absolutely not," Frank said. "I don't want to be responsible for a list of bank employees."

"Frank is correct," the attorney interjected. He gave Marge another condescending glance. "We have to consider the confidential nature of this information. Besides, I believe we have enough of a case without this. We have the credibility of the prostitute to break down."

"And if she doesn't break?" Marge asked, remembering that the police had already put pressure on her.

Frederick smiled confidently. "My job is to see that she does break," he said. "And I'm very good at my job."

CHAPTER 13

MARGE RACED UP to her apartment to call Detective Peterson, but he had already gone home. This night of all nights, she thought, he had to leave work on time. She'd have to wait for his return call in the morning.

When enough time had passed for Lori and Frank to be home, Marge phoned Lori. "Don't say anything to Frank," she said when she knew it was Lori on the line. "Come over as soon as you can without him knowing. I need to talk to you about something in private."

Lori arrived at six o'clock. "Frank went out to have a drink. He said the house was closing in on him. I told him I had to run over to the store to get something, in case he came home before I did."

Marge poured them both a cup of coffee and sat across from Lori at the kitchen table.

"Were you watching Frank's face when he read the list? I'm sure he lied. I'm sure he recognized one of the names."

"Impossible," Lori exclaimed. "From where I sat, I couldn't see his face, but if he recognized a name, he would have said something. It's too important to him not to."

"Maybe something else is more important to him at this point," Marge said. "I know this is a touchy subject, but do you by chance know the names of the women with whom Frank had affairs?"

Lori stared. "Marge, really, I don't want to drag that into this. It wouldn't look good for Frank."

"Lori, think. What if someone connected with one of those women held a grudge against Frank? Maybe a husband? What if that same person needed to frame someone for a crime? Who do you think they would choose?"

Lori looked as if she had been struck dumb. "You've got to be kidding, Marge. I know you have to stretch to come up with these theories, but this one is way out there."

"You don't have to believe me, Lori, but give me a chance to find out if I'm right. If you know the names of those two women, and if I can get Detective Peterson to show me the list or check it himself, we will know."

Lori studied her hands for a few moments. Marge took a sip of coffee and practiced deep breathing until Lori nodded her head.

"All right," she said. "Their names were Toni Blessings and Rachel Tomkins. I don't know their husband's names."

"Good," Marge said. "Now, you can forget all about it unless I find a match. I already have a call in to Pete. He probably won't let me see the list, but there is no reason he wouldn't check the names."

Lori rose immediately. "I have to go to the store in case Frank gets home before I do," she said and almost ran out the door.

"Drive carefully," Marge called after her, wishing she

could keep her here until the threat of tears had abated. "Call me when you get home."

She didn't think Lori had heard her or, if she had, that she would comply.

Marge had to hurry to get to church in time for Bible Study. The prospect of seeing Kevin, and knowing he was waiting for her, made it impossible to consider not going, even though she was so preoccupied with Lori and Frank she was afraid she would get nothing out of the discussion.

As she was about to leave the house, the phone rang. "I'm home," Lori said, and hung up.

Kevin met her at the church doorway, his face lighting up when he spotted her. "I began to think you weren't coming," he said in greeting.

Marge felt a smile spread over her face and tried to keep it in check. It didn't do to be too eager, especially when the thought of spending more time with him gave her a case of the jitters. She needed to slow this down. She wasn't sure she even wanted it to go any further. Was it because she was too attracted to him? Was she letting her fear of involvement destroy any chance for a relationship?

"I had a busy day," she said. "I found a part-time job in a framing shop. I started yesterday."

"Good for you. What about a congratulatory coffee after the meeting tonight? Before you get so busy with work that you don't have time for me again?"

"No, I can't tonight. Honest," she added when Kevin's face clouded over. She wasn't up to sorting out her feelings tonight. Too much had happened in the last two days. "How about next Sunday we have that picnic you've been suggesting? It will have to be after my art class, in the afternoon."

A smile immediately brightened Kevin's face. "Excellent," he said. "It's a date."

Marge couldn't help shaking her head as they entered the church. Kevin was so attractive, and obviously attracted to her. His attention excited her; but left her frightened and breathless. She was glad she had put off their date for a few days. She had to think this relationship and her feelings through or she could end up either getting hurt or, worse, hurting Kevin. He didn't deserve that.

When she arrived home, Marge dragged herself to the studio to start painting for the arts and crafts fairs. She didn't think she could concentrate tonight, but once she started, everything else dropped from her mind. Painting appeared to be excellent sleep therapy. By the time she fell into bed, even though worrisome thoughts fluttered around the edges of her consciousness, sleep claimed her before they could gain hold.

IT WAS AFTER nine the next morning and Marge was preparing to go to the frame shop when Detective Peterson called.

"Don't hang up until you hear me out," Marge said, remembering his penchant for cutting their conversations short. "I have the names of two women with whom Frank Knowles had an affair. I want to know if their last names appear on the list of bank employees. Frank saw the list in his attorney's office yesterday and swears he didn't recognize any of the names, but I know he's lying. He had a strong reaction to one name on the list."

"Okay, okay. You made your point," Pete said. "I won't even ask what you were doing at the attorney's office. What are their names?"

"Toni Blessings and Rachel Tomkins."

"I don't have the list in front of me. I'll call you back when I've checked these names against it."

"I'm working until two o'clock. Call me after that."

"Working? I thought you were off this week."

Didn't her police tail keep him updated? "I found a part-time job at a frame shop near here. I have to go now. Please call soon after two."

Marge worked fast and furious. It was the only way to keep from going crazy. As a result, the last framing jobs she completed were those that had come in last Friday. If she did as well tomorrow, she would be able to erase the backlog by early next week. Joshua's beaming smile, which lit up his craggy face, was all the reward she needed for the achievement.

"I am receiving some very good feedback about your work," he said as she prepared to leave.

"I love doing this," Marge said. "I hardly consider it work."

"We should be able to arrange some flexible hours if you need to find a second job. I can use your framing expertise any time of the day."

The exchange caused Marge to leave the shop later than she intended; but Detective Peterson hadn't called by the time she arrived home. She sat by the phone, waiting for it to ring. Her mind skittered from one thing to another; she knew she wouldn't be able to concentrate on anything until she found out if her hunch was right.

It finally rang at three-thirty. "I'm sorry, but no cigar," Pete said. Marge was speechless. How could that be? Frank had lied, she knew he had definitely recognized a name on that list. What else could possibly be going on in his life that would cause him to lie?

"Are you still there?" Pete asked. Marge thought she heard smugness in his words. He was probably delighted she had finally been proven wrong.

"I'm here," Marge said, her voice sounding small. "I don't understand it though. I know Frank was lying. He recognized a name on that list. On the third page."

"The third page. Hmmm. That's a list of employees who left their jobs in the last six months. So, if he recognized a name on page three, it isn't someone currently working at the bank."

"That makes sense," Marge said. "I imagine the embezzler would quit the bank before the missing funds could be traced to him, and I'm convinced the embezzler is also the murderer." She desperately wanted to look at the list herself—as if that would make one of the names she had given Pete magically appear on it. She shook her head. Even if Frank had recognized a name, since it wasn't one of the two Lori gave her, Marge had no way of knowing which one it was or why he had reacted to it.

"I don't suppose there is any way you can check out all the people listed on the third page to see if you can find a connection with Frank. Or at least narrow it down to which ones had access to the trust funds." She knew the detective's answer before he spoke.

"On what basis? That you saw Frank look at his wife while he was reading the list? Come on, Marge, the police department already has enough to keep its days full; it doesn't need wild goose chases. Especially when it means treading on the public's right to privacy."

Marge hung up the telephone, feeling as if she had been put through a wringer. How could she get around this one? And, if Frank was willing to risk going to prison for a murder he didn't commit, why should she care? Because

Lori and the children would suffer right along with Frank, that's why.

Was Frank protecting someone?

She went into the studio and put a fresh sheet of paper on the easel. Without thinking, what emerged was Frank's face, his eyes narrowed and aimed in the direction Lori had been sitting. No, the Frank Marge was beginning to know would not risk his life for someone else. If Frank's attorney didn't get him off, she was sure Frank would reveal the name of the person and his connection to that person.

ON FRIDAY, even while her mind stayed busy trying to figure out the puzzle of Frank and the name on the list, Marge worked her way through the backlog of framing projects. The front of the store was busier today, too, which not only cut into her framing time, but also added to the number of jobs to do. Marge was glad she had made such headway—and was also happy to see more work coming in. It meant job security.

When she got home, Marge went to the bedroom, opened her closet doors wide, and sat on the edge of the bed, feeling too discouraged about Frank to get excited over her evening out with Melissa. The forest-green edge of a swingy skirt caught her eye. She felt a smile tug the corners of her mouth. She used to wear that skirt when she and Gene felt a need to enliven their lives a bit. They would hire a babysitter and go on a date. He'd select a lounge with a band playing the good old songs, and they would dance until the band shut down.

She rose and started digging through the closet. Where

was that clingy blouse Gene had liked so much? She hadn't been able to wear it for years, but it hadn't mattered because their nights out disappeared as the children grew. Switching her search to the dresser, she found the blouse stuffed at the back of one of the drawers. Pulling off her shirt and slipping the blouse over her shoulders, she looked in the mirror. The green eyes looking back at her widened in surprise. It fit perfectly, skimming her hips barely below the waist.

After refreshing the skirt and blouse with an iron, Marge pulled on a pair of pantyhose and rummaged around in the closet to find her black sling-back shoes, discovering she had to dust them off before she could wear them. She pulled her auburn curls back, letting them halo out behind a green headband.

Melissa gave an appreciative whistle when Marge opened the door. "Well, whistle right back," said Marge, who had never been able to get out a decent catcall. Melissa was decked out in skinny black pants, strappy sandals, and a deep V-neck that accented her long, crocheted, electric-blue sweater. Her dark blonde hair usually hung around her shoulders; tonight it was pulled back into a gentle knot with loose tendrils framing her face.

"I knew we were overdue for a night on the town," Melissa said as she backed her Cougar into the street. "We'll be lucky if we don't get picked up in these outfits."

Marge, flashing back to her adventure on the Aurora Strip with Lori, had to stifle a giggle. Her difficulty knowing how to handle a relationship with a man intruded. "Have you ever been picked up?" she asked.

"No, I don't spend much time in bars and I'd never expect to find Mr. Right there," Melissa said. "When I find someone interesting, it is through work or activities." She glanced sideways at Marge. "What about that hunk you were having dinner with the other night?"

Marge grinned. "We're good friends, nothing more," she said, relieved to have put her jealousies aside. For a short while, she had thought David might be her next Mr. Right. And, then there was Kevin. How could you ever know? "After you've met someone, if you are both interested and you go out, what do you do?"

Melissa laughed. "You mean, do you 'go all the way,' as they said when we were in school? Not on the first date, for sure. And only if you're comfortable enough with him to make sure you are protected. Otherwise, whatever works for you."

Marge looked at Melissa out of the corner of her eye, wondering if her friend really practiced that. Marge knew it wouldn't work for her. She knew she would be considered a relic by many, but she had been a virgin when she married Gene. To her surprise, he said he was, too. That made their intimacy special in a way she didn't think would have been possible otherwise. While she'd never be a virgin again, if she had another intimate relationship she'd want to share that same kind of commitment.

Marge shrank back against the seat. She had been tempted, though, when she had felt neglected by Gene. Thank God she hadn't carried through with the temptation.

Breaking the silence, Melissa asked, "How are Frank and Lori doing?"

Marge frowned. "It is really strange. Frank lied yesterday about something that I think could be crucial to his case. I can't figure out why he would do that."

"It must be important for him to take that big a chance."

"Well, that fool attorney of his has Frank convinced he'll win the case without it. I think he wants the case to go to trial so he can strut his stuff."

"Is it something Frank wouldn't want Lori to know?"

"The way he glanced at her out of the corner of his eye when he recognized it, I'm sure that's the problem. It's a name . . . I had Pete check the names of the women Frank had affairs with against the list of bank employees. They weren't there."

"How does this name connect to the case?"

"I think a bank employee was embezzling money from dormant accounts. While Roddeman might have begun to suspect someone, I think whoever it was also wanted to hurt Frank. I don't think it had anything to do with Frank's mother's trust account except as part of the plan to trap Frank. If I'm right, killing Roddeman may have been more about hurting Frank than about the embezzlement. I'm trying to find out what bank employee would have a reason to want to hurt Frank."

"Whew," Melissa said. "You seem to have it all worked out. How does your Detective Peterson feel about all this?"

Marge shrugged. "He looked for the names of the two women, but they weren't on the list of bank employees. I tried to talk Pete into investigating other names on the list, but he thinks I've stretched what we know a little too far."

"I'm surprised he's listened to you as much as he has."

"If it makes sense and might help the case, he listens. He may be stubborn, but he's honest and cares about finding the truth."

Melissa looked at Marge out of the corner of her eye as they left the car to enter the bar.

"Don't give me that look. Pete and I have tried to work together in order to get to the bottom of this case, but we always end up angry at each other. We're too different to ever get along."

Melissa was right about getting hit on. They started with a glass of wine in a small, quiet bar where they thought they could talk. Evidently not small and quiet enough, because they had to refuse offers of drinks, which would have led to conversation and complications. Despite the interruptions, Marge filled Melissa in on her new part-time job and Melissa informed her that the real reason they were out tonight was to celebrate a huge house sale she had finalized.

"Do you always draw this much attention when you go out?" Marge asked.

"Me? What about you?" Marge looked up in surprise, only to see a pair of eyes staring at her over Melissa's shoulder. "You're not a demure little housewife anymore," Melissa continued. "That is, if you ever were. You must know your coloring, with that auburn hair, creamy complexion, and green eyes are enough to make any woman green herself with envy. Throw in those adorable freckles, and you look good enough to eat."

"Adorable? Freckles? Come on!" Marge objected.

The man staring at Marge seemed ready to pounce. "Let's get out of here," Marge said. "Is there any place two women can have a drink in peace?"

"I'm sorry," Melissa said. "I thought this early we would have the place to ourselves. Let's just go to a restaurant and relax over dinner."

"I wonder how Frank met his women," Marge said after they were seated in the glow of candlelight at the restaurant. She spoke softly even though the tables were spaced to allow private conversation. "I know the two women he had affairs with were married. You'd think he would have found women on his business trips, when he was alone in a bar, but they lived here. Most of the time he spent with them, however, was when they found some way to accompany him on his business trips."

"You know a lot about them," Melissa commented.

"Lori told me most of what she found out. Once Frank had admitted an affair, he didn't want to talk about it, but she seemed to need to know. She'd keep after him and pry as much information out of him as she could. In order to save his marriage, he finally answered most of her questions."

"So, he never volunteered that he was having an affair? Out of guilt or anything? Some men do that."

"No, he only admitted to it after Lori found out."

"So, there could be other affairs Lori doesn't know about?" Melissa asked.

Marge stared at her. "Of course. Why didn't I think of that? But it must have been hovering in the back of my mind or I wouldn't have asked Pete to keep investigating those names."

The waiter approached and they gave their dinner orders.

As soon as he was gone, Melissa asked, "Did Pete do it? Sounds like he might listen to you more than you admit."

"No, of course he didn't. But if the name Frank recognized was from an affair that Lori doesn't know about, especially since Lori told him that another affair would be the end of their marriage, he has reason to try and hide it. And, he would feel no necessity to disclose it because his attorney is positive he already has the case in the bag."

Although Marge's mind was racing, she forced herself

to relax and enjoy the shrimp cocktail followed by filet mignon. There was nothing she could do until tomorrow.

"I may never fit into these pants again," Melissa complained as they staggered to the car after refusing the dessert tray. "How could we have eaten so much?"

"One bite at a time."

They laughed and groaned all the way home.

"Let me know how you make out with your detective tomorrow," Melissa said when she dropped Marge off.

Marge shook her head as she hurried into the apartment building. Exactly how was she going to convince Pete to listen to her latest theory?

CHAPTER 14

"BE THERE, BE THERE, be there," Marge chanted from the moment her eyes popped open at five o'clock in the morning until it was late enough to call Detective Peterson. Did he even work on Saturdays? "Be there, be there, be there," accompanied her shower, her coffee, her sporadic attempts to clean house, her hovering over the telephone until nearly nine, so that by the time she heard, "Pete Peterson here," it sounded like an answer to a prayer.

Marge charged ahead, "Detective Peterson, you have to check the names on that third page. Frank Knowles had two affairs Lori knows about. That doesn't mean he didn't have others she doesn't know about. "

The sigh at the other end of the line was loud. "Marge Christensen, you are enough to try any man's patience. Can't you admit you were wrong, for once?"

"Detective Peterson . . . Pete . . . please believe me. I

wasn't wrong. When Frank read that page, his face paled. He slid a quick guilty look at Lori. His hands clutched the paper so hard his knuckles turned white. It was important to him not to admit he knew one of those names because it would mean the end of his marriage."

"You may have a point, Marge. But if Knowles won't own up to knowing someone on the list when it's in his best interests to do so, I don't think there is much we can do about it."

Marge recognized Pete's tone and knew it would be useless to argue. "I'm sorry to have bothered you," she said and hung up.

Biting her lip and pacing in a circle, Marge considered her next step. Lori usually worked on Saturday mornings. Marge could talk with her at her office while she was out of Frank's hearing. She picked up the phone but put it down quickly. Could she do this? Could she be the one to put in motion the end of Lori's marriage? Even to save the husband Lori would no longer have the choice of leaving if he were in prison? And even if Marge's hunch were true, would Lori ever forgive her?

She picked up the phone again, but instead of dialing Lori's office, she called the house. Frank picked up the phone.

"Frank, this is Marge. I have to talk with you. I don't want to do it in front of Lori, and I think you know why."

She heard a quick intake of breath. "Marge, why don't you get out of our lives?" he asked, his voice thin.

"*Now,* Frank. Meet me at Starbucks at Factoria Square." Marge hung up before he could object. She hoped he would come.

When she arrived at Starbucks, Frank was already

sprawled on a chair, all knees and elbows, with a tall latte in front of him. His eyes narrowed as she sat across from him with a cappuccino. "What do you think you know now?" he asked. His voice sounded tight and unsure despite the belligerence of the words.

"I know you recognized a name on that printout from the bank," she said, and saw confirmation in the flash of fear in Frank's eyes and the tightening of his lips. "I suspect you don't want to admit it because it could end your marriage. You had another affair, didn't you? And not with Tracy Generas. With someone on that list. Or someone whose husband's name is on that list."

"You'd better not be parading this theory to the whole world," Frank said. "If Lori hears it, it won't matter if it's true. You are correct that it will be the end of my marriage."

"And what will going to prison do for your marriage?"

"That won't happen. My attorney is one of the best, and he says they don't have enough to convict me." He grinned, but there was no joy in it. "Partly because of the doubts you've been able to raise."

"Frank, unless your attorney can break Tracy Generas, you have nothing, even with all of my fine theories. And Tracy is afraid. The police haven't been able to get anywhere with her. Whoever did this covered all the bases. Do you really expect a jury to believe that story about the motel room? Besides, think about it. If your attorney does break Tracy's story and you are exonerated, the police will be looking for the killer again. They will find him and the whole truth will come out eventually. You're going to have to accept that Lori will find out about the affair one way or another. Someone was out to get you and I think you know why."

"Who says he's the killer? What kind of logic does it take to frame a man for murder because he slept with your wife?"

"Not sane logic," Marge admitted, secretly pleased at his slip. As she had thought, it wasn't a woman on the list; it was the woman's husband. "But, crazier things have happened. You don't have to tell me anything. All you have to do is let the police know the name. Let them check it out. Don't you think it's in everyone's best interests to get a killer and embezzler off the streets and out of the banking business? I know he is no longer with First Bank. His name was on the third page, the one that listed former employees. But, so far there is nothing to keep him from getting another job in banking."

Frank stirred his coffee, not looking up. His shoulders had slumped while Marge talked. His head began to shake.

"I can't do it. I can't do it to Lori."

"You already did it to Lori. You just haven't admitted it yet," Marge corrected. "And if you did it this time, as much as you claim you want to make your marriage work, what makes you think you won't do it again? If you're not already in prison, that is. Face it, Frank. Your marriage is probably over. You've seen to that. Lori won't leave as long as you're in trouble, but after this is finished it will be a different story. Why don't you at least save your own life and save your family the pain of seeing you convicted of murder?"

Frank raised his eyes to Marge's. They were the saddest eyes she had ever seen, and she didn't think it was an act. "I really do love her, you know," he said. Marge could only nod. The words seemed to come from the bottom of his soul, but she couldn't understand that kind of love.

He pulled out a cell phone and handed it to Marge, who dialed Detective Peterson's number.

"Pete Peterson here," she heard. She didn't think she had ever been so happy to hear someone's voice.

"Marge Christensen," she replied. "I have someone who wants to talk with you."

Frank took the phone back. "The third page," he said. "The second name. Joseph Browning. He is the husband of a woman I was seeing for a little while, about three months ago. Then she disappeared." He handed the phone back to Marge.

"Pete?"

"Yes, Marge. So, you were right again."

"Pete, what are you going to do?"

"Well, it's Saturday, which complicates things; but I'm going to find the bank examiner and give him this information so he can trace the accounts this guy had access to. I'm sure the bank manager will also be glad to come in on a Saturday to start checking records. While I'm driving to the bank, I'll be using my cell phone to get people to trace any banking records this guy has anywhere else. Someone in Seattle will pick up Tracy Generas and her pimp to ask them nicely about this Browning character. With as much ammunition as I can gather, I'm going to confront Browning and wrest a confession of embezzlement, murder, and a frame up. Anything else I can do for you?"

"You don't have to be sarcastic. I know I could be wrong about him being the killer. But, Pete, will you please let me know what you find out? Lori is a very good friend of mine, and she's going to be hurt. I want to be able to help her if I can . . ." her voice lowered to a whisper. ". . . if she'll even see me."

Marge hit the button to end the call and handed the phone back to Frank. "I'm sorry, Frank. But if this man isn't the killer, Lori may never have to know about it. I won't be the one to tell her." She didn't believe Browning wasn't the killer, but Frank looked so depressed she couldn't help trying to make him feel better.

Frank straightened perceptibly and glared at her. "Not today," he said, "but how soon will it be before you can't help yourself? Before your certainty about what is right and proper for everyone makes you want to help Lori out of this relationship? No, Marge. Thank you very much. I know my marriage is over." His rueful smile had a hint of malice in it. "I doubt that Lori will thank you for it."

Marge tried to control her shaking as she drove home. Why was it her fault? She had started by telling the police what she knew. Isn't that what you are supposed to do? She had tried to clear Frank of the murder charges. Was that wrong, when no one else, including his attorney, appeared to be investigating what happened? Was it her fault Frank was so weak he couldn't stay out of bed with other women? Was it her fault if she found evidence Detective Peterson hadn't even been looking for?

Almost home, she turned around and headed to the framing shop, grateful for Joshua's open invitation to come in and work. Sitting in her apartment and waiting for Pete's call, wondering what was going on, would drive her crazy.

Marge was still on edge when she arrived home a little after four. She poured a glass of the wine she had opened the day she discovered the body, hoping it was still fit to drink, and slumped at the kitchen table. She looked at the clock. How long would it take for Detective Peterson to have some idea as to whether the cuckolded husband was a possible candidate for murder?

What if Browning had no connection to either the embezzlement or the murder? Would Lori find out about it anyway? Probably. She wrapped her arms across her stomach, feeling it churn with anxiety. It didn't matter that she was right or that Lori should leave Frank because of his infidelity. Being the catalyst that brought more pain down on Lori was too hard a burden to bear.

She jumped when the phone rang. It was David. His daughter was looking for a house and asked for Melissa's work number. Marge was glad for the diversion. She didn't think for a minute that was the only reason David wanted Melissa's phone number, but it solved her problem about how to get them together.

The phone rang again. "Hey, girlfriend." She recognized Janette's voice. "I hear you've got the case all but solved."

"Janette, thank God you're all right," Marge said. "When did you get out of the hospital?"

Janette laughed. "You make it sound like I was at death's door. They let me out this morning, with many thanks for my help. Although I didn't get anything out of that girl that we didn't already know."

"I want to hear all of it," Marge said. "Did Detective Peterson tell you anything when you left?"

"No, I didn't see him, since the hospital was in Seattle, not Bellevue. A very handsome uniformed officer drove me home, though. And asked when he could see me again."

"Well, I don't want to tie up the line, in case he calls. Why don't you and Eddie come out to my place next Monday for dinner and we'll share all the details? By then we should know more from Pete."

"You got it," Janette said. "I'll call Eddie. See you Monday at, oh, six or so?"

Marge agreed and hung up the phone.

Detective Peterson did not call, so after reluctantly pouring the rest of the vinegary wine down the sink, Marge went to bed. She would not learn anything tonight about what the police had done to follow up on Frank's confession.

CHAPTER 15

THE BRIGHT SUNSHINE on Sunday morning promised a beautiful day for a picnic. Marge tried to shake off the tension that a night's sleep had done nothing to dispel. She was in the car on her way to church before it dawned on her she should have prepared something for the picnic with Kevin today. Maybe she could stop on the way home from church and buy something appropriate.

Kevin's vibrant blue eyes still sent quivers down her spine. His presence beside her during the service and the knowledge that she was going to spend the afternoon with him distracted Marge from the sermon and from everything else that had been on her mind. She thought back to her conversation with Melissa and wondered if physical attraction was the key to finding Mr. Right.

Why did she care about finding Mr. Right? She was perfectly happy on her own.

"You want me to pick you up after your art class?"

Kevin asked as soon as they were out the church door. "There's no sense taking two cars to the park. How about Lake Sammamish State Park?" he added.

"Lake Sammamish sounds great." Lake Sammamish State Park was a popular Sunday afternoon spot. Marge and Gene had often taken the children there after church. "But give me your address and I'll drive to your apartment," she said. That way she wouldn't have to turn Kevin away at the door again. "What should I bring with me?"

"Not a thing. My treat. I'll be busy preparing it while I wait for you."

Kevin wrote down an address in Factoria and directions to get there, planted a quick kiss on Marge's cheek, and with a grin and a wave walked to his car.

Marge's art class was more fun than usual, partly because excitement about her afternoon dispelled some of her despondency and partly because the girls were thrilled to see their artwork professionally framed. The girls left at two o'clock, clutching what Marge knew were some of the most precious gifts their parents would ever receive.

After quickly cleaning the studio, Marge changed from her paint smock to casual slacks, shirt, and a sweater for the picnic. It felt strange going empty-handed to Kevin's house. The next time they got together she'd have to cook him a dinner to make up for his treating her. She shivered. That meant she'd have to let him into her apartment. She was afraid to think of where that might lead.

Pulling into a parking spot in front of a rundown apartment building, Marge frowned. Kevin had a good job and seemed like the fastidious type. Why did he live in such a dumpy place? Kevin must have sensed her confusion when he opened the door. He gave her that wicked, crooked grin that made butterflies dance in her stomach.

"Come on in for a minute and see how the other half lives," he said. "Remember, you have to make and save the money before you can invest it. I plan to be very rich someday, and I'm in the making and saving mode of that strategy, so I'm keeping my living expenses as low as possible."

Marge smiled, relieved to learn that the reason he lived here was to build his future security. She stepped into the apartment ahead of Kevin. The door lock snapped behind her. Turning to see Kevin remove a key from the lock, she frowned. It couldn't be opened, even from the inside, without a key.

"This must be a high-crime area to require that type of lock," she said, trying to rid herself of the uncertainty that had crept into her voice.

"Oh, a very high-crime area, indeed," Kevin said, his grin wider, his eyes alight with something that disconcerted Marge. "Have a look around."

Still, Marge wondered, why remove the key?

Kevin disappeared into what Marge presumed was the kitchen. She heard drawers opening and closing as she took advantage of his invitation to look around. The living room was stark: a thrift store sofa, two end tables, one small chair, and little else. In addition to the locked door, the emptiness made Marge uneasy. A framed photo on one of the end tables caught her eye. Her brows knit, bewilderment growing. Why would Kevin keep a snapshot of a sleeping woman? She walked over to look at another photo in a matching frame at the other end of the sofa. She froze.

It was a hand, surrounded by a blue denim cuff, sticking out of the ground. It was Luke Roddeman's hand.

The giggle from the kitchen doorway brought Marge up straight. The giggle from her first phone call. The giggle in the woods. Her muscles tensed and an electric silence filled the room.

"It took me long enough to get you alone, Marge Christensen," Kevin said, his voice—the same voice that had lulled her only moments before—now menacing. "I must be losing my touch."

Marge reached into her purse as she turned to face him. Kevin closed in on her. He sliced the strap of the purse with a large knife, causing it to fall on the floor before she could grab anything she might use to defend herself. Stumbling, Marge managed to keep her footing and side-step the jabbing knife. Struggling to hide her fear, she asked, "Why? You had Frank Knowles where you wanted him. Why muddy the waters by threatening me?"

Marge blinked as Kevin . . . no, not Kevin . . . Joseph Browning . . . stood still with a thoughtful look on his face. The calm façade was shattered by a demonic grin. "It was much too easy," he said. "I had to make it more of a challenge. Now, I think I'm finished playing games."

"And my car?" Marge asked, hoping to distract him. "What did you gain by trying to kill me?"

She was gratified when Kevin hesitated again. His look was hard and vindictive. "You wouldn't cooperate," he said. "You teased me, and avoided going out with me. You claimed you were too busy, but you had time for that other guy Thursday night. I had to punish you." He grinned and started toward her again. "I'm glad I didn't kill you. I would have missed this fun."

Marge sidestepped as Kevin lunged. "Who's that?" she asked, pointing to the picture of the woman sleeping.

"My wife," Kevin said, his voice harsh. "My dear wife,

who so easily succumbed to the wiles of that womanizer Frank Knowles." His finger traced her face in the photo. "Wasn't she beautiful? Who would have guessed she was so corrupt?"

Marge's head spun. "Was? Has something happened to her?"

Kevin's grin was back, his eyes as cold as stone. "Yes, something happened to her. I can tell you because you will soon be joining her. Everyone thinks she is away caring for her sick mother, but she isn't. She never left home. She'll never leave home again. I had to punish her, too. She'll stay in the freezer until I decide I don't need her anymore."

Frank had said she disappeared. "You're a sick man. You need help," Marge breathed as she searched for a way to escape. She quickly learned it was a mistake to take her concentration off Kevin. She narrowly missed the blade of the knife as he lunged at her again.

"That would be a sloppy way of killing me. Aren't you afraid of making a mess?" Moving backward through the room while keeping Kevin in front of her, Marge peeked into the doorway of the kitchen and down the hall to the bedroom. No other doors.

"I chose this place carefully," Kevin said, pride shining in his face as he held up his hands. "And I'm wearing gloves. Have been since I entered the house. I'm surprised you didn't notice, since you're supposed to be such a great detective. I'll be leaving no trace of me here, only you. And believe me, this time I plan on making a mess."

He feinted, then thrust the knife at Marge when she reacted. The tip of the blade jabbed into her arm before she could adjust her move. Marge felt the warm flow and knew the cut was deep.

"You forget about the miracles of modern science,"

Marge said, not allowing herself to look down or reach for her arm. "You will have left traces of DNA."

Kevin giggled. The sound again awakened visions of the scene at the park. "No. I won't. I don't live here. I rented the apartment furnished. I only came a few minutes before you arrived, to put my photographs here." He cocked his head, a contemplative look in his eyes. "How should I take your photo, I wonder? I wouldn't want to spoil those pretty little freckles. At least not before I have my picture. After that I might remove them one at a time." He pointed with the knife. Marge winced as it approached her eyes.

Kevin's face grew serious. Marge fought dizziness and tensed, flexing her knees, trying to remember the moves she had learned in her self-defense class. When Kevin swung at her again, she was ready and moved to one side while bringing her heel up and kicking out, hard. It landed solidly on his shin. She kicked at the hand holding the knife while Kevin staggered backward. The knife went skittering across the floor. Before Kevin could recover, she kicked him hard behind the knees. Kevin went down and she landed on top of him, her hands searching for the pocket where he had put the key.

He giggled again. The eerie sound made Marge lose her concentration for a second; long enough for Kevin to shove her off and jump to his feet. He had the knife back in his hand and was coming at her as she struggled to rise, feeling her strength seep out along with the blood from her wound.

"You didn't really think I'd leave the key where you could get your hands on it, did you? I know you, Marge Christensen. I studied you. I know all about your self-defense classes and your exploits after your husband's death. That's what made it interesting. If you weren't such a good challenge I might not have bothered."

Marge had her back against the wall beside the door. Kevin moved in to strike. There was no escape.

"Why in the park?" Marge broke in, trying to buy time, wondering what good it would do her. "Why did you kill Roddeman in the park?"

Kevin stepped back and shrugged, his eyes glittering as they watched her reaction. "I had been studying Roddeman, too. I knew he liked to walk there. So did my wife. She took Knowles there after they met." His eyes grew hard. "He seduced my wife in that park, you know. I followed them and saw them together.

"I bought the shovel over in Ellensburg two days earlier. No one would think to check on purchases that far away. I left it in the park Friday afternoon, with no fear anyone would find it before I used it. Then I only had to wait for Roddeman to come for his usual walk, bash him in the head, bury him, and leave. I wiped down the shovel and tossed it a short distance away. I decided to come back Saturday morning to leave Knowles' keys, in case their appointment wasn't enough evidence. I saw you discover the body. That was a real kick. I knew I didn't want it to end then, so I followed you home and to the Knowles' house Sunday morning. I barely had time to get to the park and plant his pen before you got there with his wife. I followed you to church. You were so perfect, getting yourself involved in the investigation; you might even have found me out before I could get to you."

Frank's keys. So that was what was in the plastic bag. No wonder the police zeroed in on Frank. But how did they suppose he got back to the motel without his keys?

Amusement filled Kevin's face, bringing back an echo

of the man she thought she knew. "I couldn't believe it when you went down to the strip in that amazing costume. You made it so much fun."

Marge had been inching away from Kevin during the respite. Kevin tensed again, looked ready to strike. Marge grabbed the photo of the hand and waved it in front of her while moving as close as she could get to the window. Using every bit of strength left in her, she flung the picture at the window, satisfied to hear the glass shatter.

"Help!" she screamed.

Immediate pounding made Kevin jump, his eyes growing wild.

"Police! Open up!"

"He's got a knife," Marge shouted, watching Kevin and ready to move if the opportunity came. "Break it in." The door cracked at the first impact. It wouldn't last long.

Kevin looked around like a trapped animal searching for escape; but he had planned it too well. There was no escape. He grabbed Marge when the door broke open. Marge stomped on his foot and twisted away as the policemen entered the apartment.

Thank God Pete had those policemen watching her. She'd have to remember to thank him, she thought as she sank to the floor.

CHAPTER 16

CONVERSATION DRIFTED IN and out of Marge's consciousness. Slowly her eyes opened and the voices became constant. She tried to move her arm and grimaced. A stab of pain stopped her and she realized there was a heavy bandage on it. The talking stopped. Turning her head, she saw Kate and Robert staring at her.

"Where am I? What are you doing here? What time is it?" she clamped her mouth shut to stop the spate of questions.

Kate laughed, relief in her voice. "You are in the hospital. It is six o'clock in the evening on Sunday. We're here making sure you're okay, which you are." Kate grinned. "It looks like you've solved another one, Mom."

Robert glared at Kate.

"Lori is here, too, in the waiting room," Kate continued, "but they wouldn't let anyone but Robert and me come in. Your friends Janette and Eddie are out there. And

Melissa. And that handsome David, who it seems you let Melissa take away from you." Robert glared even harder. "Even David's daughter, Susan, and her husband were here, and your pastor and a couple other church members, but they didn't want to crowd the emergency waiting room so they left. Susan and her husband will meet us later. Everyone wants to see with their own eyes that you're okay. The doctor says there's nothing seriously wrong with you; you had a shock and lost some blood. You didn't even need a transfusion, although you will have to drink a lot of liquids for the next few days. You can leave here as soon as you feel strong enough to walk.

"So, if you give Robert the apartment keys, he can take the gang over there, where everyone will be more comfortable, and I can escort you when you're ready."

It all came back to Marge in a rush. "What about Pete?" she asked. "Has he said anything yet? Has he dropped the charges against Frank?"

"Yes, he has," Robert finally spoke. "I don't know if Lori will come to your place or go home to him. Other than that, we haven't heard anything from the detective."

Marge felt strangely bereft.

Kate snorted. "If Lori's smart she'll come to Mom's and not go home until Frank has cleared out."

Marge took her purse when Robert handed it to her. "Please send Lori in when you and the others go over to the house," she said as she fished out her keys.

"Are you all right?" Marge asked Lori when Kate and Robert left.

"Of course I'm not all right," Lori snapped. "I'm not sure I'll ever be all right again."

"I'm sorry, Lori. I never dreamed . . ."

Lori sighed. "It's not your fault, Marge. You didn't have

the affair, Frank did. You kept him out of prison, like I knew you would. For the children and me, thank you."

"Are you going to be all right?" Marge repeated.

"I'll be fine . . . eventually," Lori said. "It's not as if I haven't had practice. But this time, it's for keeps. Remember how, when Gene died and I found out about Frank's first affair, you said that in a way for you it was easier because it was final? Now I know what you meant. This is final. I'm going home and telling Frank to pack and get out of the house. Tomorrow I'm filing for divorce."

"What are you going to do then?"

"Nothing. Not for awhile. I have my job, and the luxury of staying in my home until I decide. I thought about it a lot after Frank's other affairs, but I think I have to actually live alone before I can figure out what my life is with the kids gone and Frank no longer a part of it. I won't be going over to your place today; but I'll talk to you soon."

Marge stared after Lori when she left. Even though she had done her best for Lori, she was afraid their relationship would never be the same again. The loss overwhelmed her for a moment as she sat on the edge of the bed, letting regrets for the misfortunes in both their lives wash over her. Resolutely, she shook them off. When Gene died Marge found and developed strengths she hadn't known were in her. She learned to take life one day at a time, leaving the past behind, preparing for tomorrow. She learned how to be the best person she could be, on her own. Lori would discover the same things once she adjusted to being alone. Who knew? Their friendship might even grow stronger.

Marge dressed as quickly as her sore arm allowed. "Come on, Kate," she said, as she stepped out into the hall. "Let's go home." A nurse raced up and sent Marge back to her room to wait for a wheelchair.

"I thought they said I could leave as soon as I could walk," she complained, but was glad enough not to have to walk the length of the hallways to the exit.

When they reached her apartment, Marge walked in the door to a babble of conversation. She barely had time to greet everyone before the phone rang.

"Pete here," the detective announced when she answered. "I figured you deserved to hear what's happened since you were the driving force behind it."

Marge waved her hand to silence the group. "I'm putting you on speakerphone," she said as she switched it on, thankful Gene's old office phone with the extra features was still hooked up.

"I am so glad you had those policemen watching me," she said.

"I'm glad you had the presence of mind to break that window and yell," Pete replied. "We had it figured out and were on our way, but we would have been too late."

"You had it figured out? How?"

"It would have taken a lot longer if Tracy Generas hadn't been picked up again. We asked her if the jewelry was all she got from Joseph Browning for setting up Frank. She asked who Joseph Browning was. Either she was still stalling or she didn't know him by that name, so we showed her a photo of Browning.

"The different name evidently confused Tracy enough so that she blurted out the truth before she had time to think. She said the man's name wasn't Browning, it was Kevin Lewis, the man who got Jimmy to help him. She complained that she didn't have the jewelry or the money anymore. Jimmy had taken the money and Lewis made Jimmy give the jewelry back to Tracy to show the police, but the police took it away from her. She said that if Lewis had told her the police would take the jewelry, she wouldn't have made it so easy for them like he told her to. And, she confirmed that while Frank was drugged, Lewis came to the motel room and took some of his things.

"That was enough to bring Browning/Lewis in for questioning. The problem was, we couldn't find him. We got a search warrant for his house in Seattle. Imagine our surprise when we found the body of his wife stowed in the freezer. I assume he told you about this when you saw the photo in the apartment?"

"Yes, he seemed all too proud of what he had done with his wife," Marge said with a shudder. "So, how did you find the apartment?"

"We strong-armed a weekend supervisor at the telephone company into pulling up a list of Browning's calls for the last two weeks. Several were to that apartment building. When we checked with the manager, she said she had never actually seen Kevin Lewis but she gave us his apartment number. But, how did you get there?"

"Since the day after I found Roddeman's body, Kevin has been going to my church, trying to get me to go out with him. I never made the connection; but for some reason I kept putting him off. I finally agreed to go on a picnic with him this afternoon, which I thought was safe; but unfortunately I stepped into his apartment before we left for the park."

"Hmmm. Anyway, when we brought Browning in, we let him catch a glimpse of Tracy, which seemed to convince him the jig was up, because he started talking and he hasn't stopped yet. In fact, it appears he welcomes the opportunity to brag about his handiwork, from his wife's disappearance to framing Roddeman for the embezzlement—yes, including the ring and jewelry from the only safety deposit box he actually got into. He faked the phone calls not only to get Knowles into the motel room with Tracy but also to have messages from the Salt Lake City hotel forwarded to Knowles there. He thinks it was a stroke of genius to put the ring on Roddeman's finger and leave the hand sticking out of the grave so we wouldn't miss it. But he's most anxious to hear about whatever misery he caused Knowles and wants to know if Knowles' wife is still speaking to him. He actually seems to be glad he got caught so he could take credit for the whole thing.

"By the way," he added, "what's this I hear about Knowles' pen being found at the crime scene?"

"The pen? Oh, the pen. I had forgotten about that. Probably because it didn't seem to be a crime scene anymore. And it wasn't there when it was a crime scene, or you would have found it. And, Lori made me promise not to tell you." Realizing she was babbling, Marge clamped her mouth shut for a moment. "What about the pen?" she finally asked.

"It seems Browning was already following you. He guessed you were heading for the park, got there before you, and planted the pen. He wanted to make sure Mrs. Knowles had no doubt her husband had been there. He somehow finds her at fault for not keeping her husband happy at home."

"Lori's fault?" Marge heard her voice rising, so she took a deep breath to calm down. "Of course, he didn't take any blame for his wife straying." She shook her head. Men. "Poor Lori. She stood by Frank through all of this, although I think that's over now."

"Yes, well, it doesn't sound like he's any prize, even if he isn't a murderer," Pete said.

"No, but he was all Lori had. And they had a good marriage for many years. What happens to married men, anyway?"

"I wouldn't know," Pete said. "I never married."

"I'm not surprised," Marge said, taking pleasure in being the one to hang up.

Marge's struggle with Kevin Lewis had left a residue of aches and pains. Everyone wanted to talk about the case, but Marge excused herself, wrapped her bandaged arm in plastic, and took a warm shower, followed by one of the pain killers the doctor had prescribed.

She slipped into comfortable black slacks with a long-sleeved blouse in a shade of green that matched her eyes and rejoined the group in the living room, where Kate planted her in a chair and brought her a glass of tonic water.

"Sorry, no wine," Kate said. "Not until you're off those pain killers. But I promise you several bottles of whatever takes your fancy." She looked around. "Feels like a party. Maybe I should have brought a date."

Marge stared at her. "What?" Kate asked with a laugh. "You off of men now? Don't worry, I have no plans to get involved anytime soon."

Probably a good thing, Marge thought. She could only hope Kate had better instincts about the opposite sex than her mother. Spotting Robert standing alone and looking lost, she added, or her brother.

Kate crossed the room to talk with Susan and Mark, who stood together as a couple and seemed to melt into a single unit. What lay ahead for them, Marge wondered. Would their infatuation with each other withstand the disillusionment when they discovered they were two people with separate needs and wants that would have to be adjusted if they were to make a life together?

They smiled at Kate as she approached and David drifted away from his daughter, his eyes on Melissa. Marge saw Melissa's face light up when she turned to find David approaching her.

Marge frowned, wondering if she wanted these two good people to risk a serious relationship, with all the pain that could follow. She sighed. David and Melissa were old enough to know. They evidently found each other worth taking the risks for. Would she ever again find someone to whom she could entrust her happiness?

She shook her head. No, that wasn't right. She might find someone who she thought loved her and whom she loved in return, but it was up to her to safeguard her own happiness. She could never leave it in the hands of another person. Because, how could you ever know?

Janette and Eddie arrived with aroma-laden packages, reminding Marge that she hadn't eaten lunch.

"I wondered where you two were," Marge said, rising to help stow the food until they were ready to eat. Their arrival sparked more conversation about the case. The other young people gathered around, eager for information. With David and Melissa off to themselves, Marge began to feel like a chaperone at a youth gathering.

"How in the world did you get the guy to confess?" Janette asked, clearly delighted to have been involved in a small part of the case.

"He seemed only too happy to boast about how clever he was when he thought I was going to be his next victim. Later, Pete worked his magic, with well-placed innuendo and leading questions. Pete somehow made everyone open up and start talking once he had the whole picture."

"It wouldn't have worked if the guy hadn't been so eager to brag about his masterful scheme."

Marge looked around to see Pete standing behind her and realized she had been waiting for him. "Your son let me in," he continued. "I'm sorry to barge in on your party. I came to see how you were doing."

"Oh, stay for dinner," Kate said. "We've ordered a ton more food than we can eat." The offer of free food seemed to sway him.

With the kids talking amongst themselves, Pete joined Marge in the kitchen. His help with setting out the dishes and utensils kept Marge from having to move around too much. They worked together with the ease of long practice. Marge caught a baleful glare from Robert when she laughed at something Pete said.

The young people left early. Kate, Susan, and Mark appeared to be making plans with Janette and Eddie for meeting up the next weekend at a lounge in downtown Seattle that was featuring a band they all enjoyed.

Robert came to say good-bye. Marge could hold back no longer. She reached out to his tall frame and pulled him close to her.

"I know you're hurting, honey," she said. "If there is anything I can do, you only need to tell me."

"Thanks." Robert's voice was gruff. "I don't think there's anything anyone can do right now; the damage has already been done. But, I might need to crash with you for a few days."

"You're sure that's the way to go?" she asked.

"What else?" Robert said. "I don't know why I didn't see it a long time ago. Caroline's so full of herself she can't see or care about anyone. Her insisting that she will have an abortion at the slightest hint of a problem, and not even feeling bad about it, and then getting her tubes tied so she wouldn't get pregnant again! That was the last straw. I can't live with that kind of selfishness any longer. I'll be seeing an attorney next week. The only thing we have to work out is property division, since we both have good jobs."

Marge wanted to talk more, but what could she say? Robert and Caroline were on opposite ends of the pole and Marge didn't see any way for them to work it out. Nor, in all honesty, did she want them to. It had never felt like Caroline was part of the family, and Marge couldn't stand the misery in which Robert had been living since he married her. But she knew it wasn't all one sided. Caroline was not as unfeeling as Robert made her out to be; Marge had seen that for herself.

Marge felt another stab of pain in the corner of her heart that had been reserved for her first grandchild. She gave Robert one more hug before he turned and left the apartment.

"Should I leave you alone with the lovebirds?" Pete asked.

David and Melissa drifted to the door. "I think we should go, too," David said, and Melissa looked at Marge with wonder on her face.

"I amend that," Pete said after they left. "May I stay and help you, since everyone else seems to have abandoned you?"

Marge suddenly felt too tired to face the clearing up that had to be done tonight. "Yes, Pete, I think I could use your help."

"That's a first," he quipped, positioning himself in front of the sink, rolling up his sleeves, and opening the dishwasher, making it apparent that he had done this before. "Usually you are busy insisting that I need yours."

Don't miss Marge Christensen's next mystery . . .

Who More Than Wished YOU WERE DEAD?

Turn the page for a preview . . .

Who More Than Wished You Were Dead?

Marge Christensen arrives at the beautiful and quiet resort town of Ocean Shores, Washington, ready to relax and paint for an entire week. Her adult children, Robert and Kate, will join her for the weekend.

Marge's plans to spend time with her children are disrupted when Robert reconnects with an old friend, Hillary Carlson, who is staying in a nearby condo with her abusive husband and his coworkers. Robert decides he will be Hillary's savior—which has serious consequences when Hillary's husband, Craig, turns up dead on the beach.

Before returning home to Bellevue, Robert asks his mother to look after Hillary's interests. Marge reluctantly agrees, hoping there will be nothing she needs to do, but the police soon zero in on the abused spouse as the best suspect. Marge doesn't have far to look for other suspects, though, since every one of Craig's coworkers has a reason to wish him out of the way. Unfortunately, the police think Robert's interest in Hillary puts him on that list, too.

With her son a suspect, Marge is doubly determined to find the murderer. In the five days at her disposal, she delves into the tangle of relationships, motives, and opportunity. And, once again, she paints a picture that leads to the surprising truth about who killed Craig Carlson.

ABOUT THE AUTHOR

PATRICIA K. BATTA, a Michigan native, attended Northwestern Michigan Community College in Traverse City, received her B.A. from the University of Puerto Rico, and finished at Oberlin College in Ohio with a Master's degree in education.

After teaching elementary students in Ohio and Pennsylvania, Batta moved to Seattle, Washington, where she lived for twenty-one years. In addition to teaching, she has worked as an editorial assistant, a document librarian, and in records management.

Batta has been writing since she was ten years old. By the time she retired, she had drafted two mystery novels and was working on a third. The first of the Marge Christensen Mystery Series, *What Did You Do Before Dying?* was published in 2008. The third, *Who More Than Wished You Were Dead?* will arrive in 2010.

Batta lives in Traverse City, where she is active in her church, the Love INC organization, and writing.

You may contact her via www.lillimarpublishing.com or www.patriciabatta.blogspot.com.

TO ORDER ADDITIONAL COPIES OF THIS BOOK AND OTHER MARGE CHRISTENSEN MYSTERIES, VISIT: